Mortimer Collins, Frances Cotton Collins

The Village Comedy

Mortimer Collins, Frances Cotton Collins

The Village Comedy

ISBN/EAN: 9783744792578

Printed in Europe, USA, Canada, Australia, Japan

Cover: Foto ©Andreas Hilbeck / pixelio.de

More available books at **www.hansebooks.com**

THE VILLAGE COMEDY.

BY

MORTIMER AND FRANCES COLLINS.

IN THREE VOLUMES.

VOL. I.

LONDON:

HURST AND BLACKETT, PUBLISHERS,

13, GREAT MARLBOROUGH STREET.

1878.

THE VILLAGE COMEDY.

CHAPTER I.

THE COPSE HILL INN.

Comedy meaneth sweet play in a village.
British Birds.

VALENTINE : . . . . Landlords differ, friend.
There be some put salt i' the tankard.
ORSON :   . . . . Ay, a plague to them.
They themselves drink not, so they spoil
good liquor.
Old Play.

"LET us go up this hill," said Frank Forncett to his companion, "and we shall get a good view of the country round."

Frank Forncett and his young friend, Harry Rivers, were making an autumn tramp through Oakshire, and had taken the train from London to a Thames-side town, whence they had begun their walk.

"What a splendid view!" said Harry, as they reached the top of the knoll.

"I wish we'd brought a glass," said Frank; "we might make out some of the country."

They were standing near a clump of trees, under which some beneficent person had placed a large bench. An old man was sitting on the bench, evidently resting from the load he had been carrying. As the gentlemen approached he got up, lifted his hat most courteously, and said:

"Gentlemen, I hope I am not in your way."

Although his clothes looked ragged and old, he had no roughness in his manner, but showed a natural gentleness; and his blue eyes were so bright, and long white hair so picturesque, that Harry Rivers, who was an impetuous youth, became enthusiastic about him, and wanted to find some way of offering him money, as he thought by the appearance of his clothes he must need it. He said:

"Pray don't move. You must need rest if you have carried such a load as that up the hill. Have you far to go?"

"Not much farther, sir. But, you see, I ain't as young as I was."

"I daresay you are a good age," said Frank Forncett.

"I'm in my eighty-five," said the old man.

"Then, perhaps, you are the oldest inhabitant," said Frank; "there are generally two or three 'oldest inhabitants' about a village."

"Well, sir, now that old Webb is gone, I suppose I am about the oldest. I am older than the church and the inn and the shop, and most of the houses in the village. But that church you see over there, sir, with the tall spire, is a sight older than me, for they say it's six hundred years."

"What is the name of this village?" said Frank.

"Copse Hill, sir."

"And may I ask your name?" said Harry modestly, feeling that age should be respected.

"Leonard Day, sir; but I'm generally called Old Leonard in these parts."

"May I have the pleasure of making you a present?" said Harry, pushing five shillings into the old man's hand.

"God bless you, sir," said Old Leonard in astonishment; "you must be a most extraordinary good young gentleman."

"If you are going to act in that way to all the picturesque ragged old men you meet in villages on your way," said Frank, "you'll have to write to your father before we come to the end of our tramp and ask him for another cheque."

"But, look here," said Harry, as they made their way down the hill through yellow furze and purple heather, " what a pretty village ! Really, it is the prettiest I ever saw in my life. Just look at that inn in the broad sunlight, and the burly landlord at the door. What a picture ! and what a jolly little nest of a house there is enclosed by all those trees. And look at the village shop across the green there. What is it painted on the board ? BAKER, GROCER, DRAPER, READY-MADE CLOTHES AND HATS! I suppose that is the only shop. What a primitive place to be only thirty miles from London. How I should like to dream away my life here! I should like to live in that nest and work in the garden, and nail up the roses and honeysuckles on the walls, and never leave this peaceful spot! How I envy you, old fellow; you could do all that if you like; you are not obliged to work as I am; I hear of nothing but my career— as if I cared for a career! Why can't my father let me have enough to come and live in a cottage and be quiet?"

"My dear boy, you talk nonsense; you don't know the world yet. In calculating life you leave no room for the passions of men, either good or evil."

"But there can be no evil in such a place as this: surely everything must go smoothly here. There are no rival shopkeepers to hate one another, and the people who live in the cottages round must be good when they have such beautiful country always before their eyes. I can understand that in squalid streets, in close towns, there must be everything that is bad; but in such a lovely spot as this people cannot help being good."

"Well, let us go in and taste the village ale, and I'll bet you a cigar, Frank, that in a very few minutes I'll show you that there is as much evil speaking, lying, and slandering here as anywhere; and I'll bet another cigar that the shopkeeper and innkeeper have a quarrel."

They entered the village inn, the Pleiades.

"A fine morning, gentlemen," said Biggins, the landlord, a man of the Daniel Lambert build. There was a kind of surliness in his civility.

"Yes," said Frank Forncett, "it is a fine morning. We want to taste your ale, landlord, and perhaps you can give us a bit of bread and cheese."

"Come in, sir," said Biggins.

"Now then, some bread and cheese and ale," said Biggins to his wife, a pleasant-looking woman, who seemed rather above her position.

"Will you walk into the parlour," she said, "and it shall be brought to you."

"No, thank you," said Frank, whose idea was gossip, "it will do here."

The "bar" of the Pleiades was a small room with a bow window, which enabled you to see what was going on either up or down the road, and there was an aggressive clock over the fireplace.

Mrs. Biggins busied herself to supply the travellers' wants, and old Biggins, whose body seemed too heavy for his legs, flopped down on the window-seat, and eyed them drowsily. Harry Rivers was somewhat disappointed with what he supposed was an ideal landlord. His burly form at the doorway, seen from the hill, looked picturesque; but nearer inspection showed that his fibre was coarse and his frame heavy.

"This is a very pretty village, landlord; it is called Copse Hill, is it not?"

"Yes," said Biggins, with a grunt.

"Do you know the population of the place?" said Frank.

Biggins scarcely understood the meaning of this.

"How many people?" explained Frank.

"Well, sir," he answered slowly, "I don't know that I've ever counted, but there's a main few comes here for beer. It's a dead-and-alive sort of place, and wouldn't do me much good but for the farming and carrying."

"Oh! then you are a farmer and carrier," said Frank. "By the way, you've a famous man somewhere in these parts, I believe."

"A famous man!   I haven't heard of him," said Biggins.   "Have you?" he said, addressing his wife, as she came in with the bread and cheese.

"No," she said, "I don't know of anyone about here particularly famous.   There's Sir Herbert West and Squire Ashley, and Mr. Perivale and Captain Lovelace."

"No, I mean Mr. Manly Frowde; doesn't he live in these parts?"

"Oh, yes," said the landlady; "but he's nobody; he lives just over there in a little house behind those trees; but he's nobody at all: he keeps no carriage, and has only an odd man about the place.   We don't take him as much account, sir."

"So much for honour in one's own village, Harry," said Frank.

"Have you a post-office here?" said Frank to Mrs. Biggins.   He had noticed that the village shop was a post-office, and wanted to hear what was the landlord's opinion of the shopkeeper.

"Yes, sir," said Mrs. Biggins; "it is over at the shop there."

"They seem to sell everything there," said Frank. "Who keeps the shop?"

"Miss Tattleton," said the landlady.

"And a nice character she is," said Biggins, who suddenly sat upright, as if he had found something sufficiently worth sitting upright for. "Why, I wouldn't post a letter there for anything. Not I, I'd rather have my old mare out and trot off to Wenley to post my letter. It was all along of that there fellow who lives in there," pointing to Manly Frowde's place, "that she got that post-office. We used to have a pillar-box, and quite enough too, but that there fellow in there must have a post-office; a pillar-box ain't good enough for him. And so he writes to some of these here people up in London, and he gets just what he likes. Why, if a poor fellow gets a drop too much and makes a bit of a noise outside here, he writes to some of these here people and down come the police on us. They say now he's going to have a telegraft down here, but I shan't send no telegrafts through that busybody, Miss Tattleton, and I don't know who else will."

Biggins seemed inclined to go on, but was out of breath with such a long speech. His remarks were generally laconic, unless some one whom he considered his enemy was mentioned. At this time Miss Tattleton and Mr. Manly Frowde happened to be his chief enemies.

"I say, Harry," said Frank, quietly, "two cigars."

Harry's face had certainly lost a trifle of its sunshine.

" Cigars, sir, did you say?" put in Mrs. Biggins.

" No, thank you, we've plenty with us."

Harry quietly pulled out his case and offered it to Frank, who took two cigars with a quiet air of amusement.

As they walked away Mrs. Biggins stationed herself at the bar window to see which way they went.

" Going over to the old cat, I suppose," grunted Biggins. " Don't think much of them gents."

" The eldest one was no gentleman, I should say," observed Mrs. Biggins, " for he wears almost as shabby a coat as that Frowde."

" Perhaps they've come after the silver spoons," said Biggins.

"There they go into the shop," said Mrs. Biggins.

"A nice lot of lies she'll tell 'em," said the landlord.

CHAPTER II.

THE COPSE HILL SHOP.

O gossip, thou delicious thing !
  Thou tirest not, like love or liquor :
When there's a story with a sting
  How shrill tongues move, how green eyes flicker !

"WELL, Harry, what do you think of your ideal village landlord ?" said Forncett.

"He certainly does not seem to be living in charity with his neighbours, but then he may be an exception. Perhaps we shall find the shopkeeper more amiably disposed. Good morning," he said to a middle-aged, brisk-looking woman who opened the shop door as the two gentlemen approached.

The door was divided in two, and humble customers squeezed through half as best they might, but when Miss Tattleton saw anyone of consequence coming, she generally unbolted the other half, and gave a courteous greeting. Though not always might the greeting be courteous: it would partly depend on the day of the week. Miss Tattleton was occasionally visited by commercial gentlemen, who prowl from place to place with long faces and long bills, and whose faces elongate if they do not happen to receive precisely the sum of money they expect, since they know that their employers will visit on them the sins of their customers.

Miss Tattleton gave long credit to villagers, which was perhaps worse for them than for herself, as when once they had run up a heavy score they found it almost impossible to pay it quite off. Still, as she would observe, the poor things must not starve, and no doubt she saved many a family from going on the parish in the time of their distress. Then when there were weeks of frost in winter, or wet weather in summer, half the parish would be taking credit from the village shop, hoping for better days soon.

Miss Tattleton's travellers did not share her sympathy with the poor, but only wanted their money, and she, in disgust, nicknamed them "fiends." Therefore, should you go to her shop when she has had a visit from a fiend, you will not find her in a good temper. Her dormant cynicism will be developed. She will not have a good word for anyone, and will describe all her neighbours in unpolished epigrams.

Miss Tattleton to-day is radiant. It is a good harvest, her poor customers are bringing in money, and there is plenty for any fiend that may turn up. Besides, she sees a couple of strangers, and anything new is her delight. Dressed in a bright cotton dress, and pleased with herself and all the world, she looks twenty years younger than she probably is.

"Good morning, sir," she said, in answer to Harry's greeting. "Will you take seats, gentlemen?"

"No, thank you," said Harry, who at once sat on the counter, and began surveying the contents of the shop.

It was a small room with a counter on each side, where were draperies and groceries of all sorts; cheese, butter, lard, eggs, sweets, corduroys, smockfrocks, gaiters, crockery, tin-ware; and from the ceiling hung brooms and brushes, boots and shoes, candles, gridirons, tea-pots, saucepans, and many other things.

"What a curious mixture," said Harry.

"You can get everything you want, from a rasher of bacon for breakfast to a candle to light you to bed."

"Yes, sir, and some paper and envelopes to write to your sweetheart," said Miss Tattleton. "But don't you want something of this sort?" and she handed him a pair of baby's socks. She always has a touch of impertinence, sometimes pleasant, and sometimes spiteful.

"I am rather too old to wear them," said Harry, "and too young to want them for somebody else."

"There would be no harm in having a pair ready," said Frank, who entered into the fun of the thing. "Your time must come."

"It doesn't come to everyone," said Miss Tattleton, "or I should be a grandmother by now; but what can I serve you with?"

"I have come for some postage stamps,

and to know whether you have any bad people in these parts," said Frank.

"Postage stamps are plentiful, but bad people are scarce. We are a very well-behaved village : the parson works so hard that they think of making him a bishop, the school-master talks Latin, the innkeeper sells good beer, and never uses bad language, and as for myself I try to prevent gossip. There's somebody across the way who writes books and never puts any of us into them, though there is great temptation, as we are a queer lot." Miss Tattleton thought herself great at irony.

"What a jolly place this must be to live in," said Rivers. "Is there a cottage to let?" he said, jokingly, "with just room to swing a cat in."

"We don't allow swinging cats in this village. You would not swing that beauty, would you?" pointing to a magnificent mouser, with long fur, too lazy to open her eyes.

"If I tried, her mistress might scratch, if she didn't. But how about a cottage?" said Rivers.

"I have heard that the gentleman who lives across the lane there is going away. He wants to marry a few daughters, and young men are scarce about here."

"Now, Forncett, wouldn't that place suit you? You might take the house and one of the daughters as well, and I could come and stay with you."

"Is that house really to be let?" said Frank Forncett, seriously.

"Well, sir, I had it from the coachman, as had it from the lady's-maid, that the family thinks of going to live near London to bring the youngest young lady out. They haven't put up a notice to let, but I've heard they have employed an agent, and I know people have been coming to see it, so there would be no harm in inquiring."

"And so your neighbour opposite writes books?" said Frank; "but I suppose none of you read them."

"I don't read his rubbish," said Miss Tattleton; "but I'm told he puts me in his books and says I keep a scandal-shop. I gave him a bit of my mind one day, and told him he was ruining my business by saying that. At our 'Penny Readings' he reads a lot of foolish verses about the people here, and fancies he is going to keep us all in order, though I do think he has improved the language of the landlord over the way, who used to swear awful till Mr. Frowde made fun about it at a penny reading."

"But I thought you were all such good people, and that there was no swearing or slandering or anything wrong. In such a lovely peaceful little place as this you ought to live like a happy family," said enthusiastic Harry.

"You had better come and show us the way, sir," answered Miss Tattleton.

"And who lives in that house?" said Frank Forncett, pointing to a good-sized red-brick house lying opposite to the left, behind a couple of acres of meadow.

"Oh, that is Mrs. Selfe's. She is a very queer old lady. She has two pretty daughters, but she treats them so badly they won't live with her. So there she is in that big house all by herself. She has got a different religion from us, but she comes to church sometimes, and always sits down at the parts about Jesus Christ and the Holy Ghost. She never spends any money in the neighbourhood, or does anything for anybody; so the sooner she goes the better. Her daughters come to visit Mrs. Manly Frowde, and the old lady don't like to have her own flesh and blood so near her; so they say she's going, and that will be another house to let, which perhaps might suit you, sir," said Miss Tattleton, turning to Harry Rivers.

"But I shouldn't know what to do with such a big house all to myself," said Harry.

"Oh! you could easily find some one to share it with you. There are a great many young ladies in these parts wanting husbands. Why, Mr. Urgent, the Vicar of Battlefield, has eight grown-up daughters, and only one is married. She has just married her father's curate; you might choose anyone of the other seven."

"Perhaps you'll choose for me," replied Harry.

"They're all such beauties that if I was a gentleman I should not know which to choose," said Miss Tattleton.

" And who is your clergyman here?" said Frank Forncett.

" Mr. Bonfellow, sir, and a downright good fellow he is. People do complain of him sometimes, but they are never satisfied. They say he takes too many holidays, and then the old men and women have to die without him, which they don't think right; and they say he gives to people who want, whatever they are, whether they are chapel people, or drunkards, or anything else bad; and he will even help a woman in distress who has got a baby without first getting a husband, and there are plenty of that sort about here."

" Shocking," said Frank Forncett; " you wouldn't help such a creature, would you?"

" Of course not," said Miss Tattleton, with mock gravity. Though Miss Tattleton has been known to nurse a man in delirium tremens, when his wife and all his friends were frightened to go near him; and she never flinches when she is asked to go and sit up with a fever or small-pox patient. She does not deny help to the worst of characters, and would assist her greatest enemy if he were in distress. To the woman with a baby and without a husband she would no doubt give a severe scolding —and some clothes for the baby.

"Do you know if Mr. Bonfellow is related to Sir Richard Bonfellow?" said Frank.

"Yes, sir; he is his youngest son."

"Ah! I know the old gentleman," said Frank, turning to Harry, "and a grand old boy he is!"

"Well, madam," said Frank, who treated all women respectfully, "I will take my postage stamps and depart. Perhaps I shall have the pleasure of seeing you again some day."

"I hope so, sir," she replied, and she bowed them out.

"What nice fellows!" she said to her niece, Susan, who had been upstairs putting on her afternoon gown, but had been down for the last five minutes watching them through the little parlour window that looked into the shop.

"What a swell the young one looked! The old one looks more like Mr. Frowde's sort, in his shabby old coat," said Susan.

"Yes, but do you know," said her aunt, "that I believe the old one means to go and look at old Wemys's house, and I shouldn't be surprised if he took it; for he said he might have the pleasure of seeing me again, and he seems to know old Dick's father."

Old Dick was Miss Tattleton's way of speaking of the Rev. Richard Bonfellow. She had such nicknames for most of her neighbours.

"I shouldn't have thought he was much, from his clothes, aunt."

"I didn't at first, but I could soon see he was a real gentleman," said Miss Tattleton, who fancied she was clever at discerning true gentlefolk, though if she had been questioned she would hardly have been able to say what her standard of gentility was. Most people of her class, and also a much higher class, fix it a carriage and pair of horses. The pair is necessary—one horse would not do. A pony-chaise or a gig may mean respectability, but a true gentleman or lady must have a pair of horses. Now Miss Tattleton was somewhat of a Radical in this matter: she would pay deference to anyone who arrived at her shop in a carriage-and-pair, but she would express her free opinion of them all the same. "Mean wretches!" she exclaimed of one family, as they went from her shop; "they try to beat everybody down, and get everything as cheap as they can, and begrudge their servants a bit of extra tea and sugar, and all to keep a pair of horses in front of them. I don't call them real gentlefolks."

A customer came into the shop. She was a flighty-looking young person from the village inn. Miss Tattleton knew that this young woman never came into her shop except as an excuse for asking questions, so she fancied—and rightly—that the two strangers who had just left were the objects of curiosity.

"I want an 'air-net and a yard of elastic," said the young person, simperingly. "What lovely weather, Miss Tattleton. I have just been for a little walk, and I met two gentlemen going into Wemys's house. I suppose they are friends of Mr. Wemys. They had lunch at our house."

The truth was that Mrs. Biggins had told

her daughter to walk up the road and watch where the two gentlemen went when they left Miss Tattleton's.

Miss Tattleton was shrewd enough to guess this, and knew that the young woman wanted to know all about them.

" No, they're no friends of his. They've been sent down here by the Government to inquire about the water. So they came to me first to know what I had to say, and now they have gone to Mr. Wemys."

" But mamma said they were quite strangers, and knew nothing about anyone in the place, and hardly knew the name of the place."

"Of course not," said Miss Tattleton, "because they've never been here before; but I daresay they'll come again, and you'd better tell your mother's man to look out, for they'll be down upon him."

The young woman tossed her head proudly, and quickly retreated, making up her mind not to visit Miss Tattleton again in a hurry. Which resolution she would no doubt keep till curiosity should overcome pride.

"I've settled her for a time," said Miss Tattleton, as she wiped her spectacles, preparatory to settling down to her accounts.

The fact was that Biggins, who would at any time cut off his nose to spite his face, had, at some trouble to himself, diverted the course of a brook which from time immemorial had supplied water to various houses in the village. It was Miss Tattleton's sole water-supply; and after passing through her garden, it ran into Mr. Wemys's grounds, and formed a dip for the use of his gardener. Miss Tattleton offended Biggins by pointing out to the sanitary inspector some nuisance on his premises: he, in revenge, caused holes to be dug in the chalk to let the rivulet off, so that no water passed beyond his own farm, and many families were inconvenienced. Mr. Wemys, who was especially annoyed, took action in the matter, but through the unsatisfactory state of the law obtained no redress. Biggins lost about fifty pounds over the litigation, and would probably in time have been brought to his senses, but Mr. Wemys, having decided to leave the neighbourhood, took no more trouble about it.

CHAPTER III.

THE HOUSE TO LET.

Love you the man, with fine loquacious vein,
Who pours small beer of talk as if 'twere dry champagne ?

"SHE'S an odd character," said Frank Forncett, as he and Harry Rivers walked across the green from the village shop. At this moment a tall man passed through the gate of Mr. Manly Frowde's house, and lounged up the road reading a book. He wore an old velvet coat and a white waistcoat, and a battered straw hat with a red ribbon round it. The book he

was reading seemed centuries old, with its
yellow pages, and oak cover, and antique
clasps.   The little green opposite the village
shop forms a triangle, and as Frank and
Harry reached a corner of it they came close
to the stranger.   He had just closed his
book, and seemed to be repeating something
from it to himself, quite unconscious that
anyone was near him.

"This is Manly Frowde, I am sure," said
Frank.   "Let us pay reverence to genius."
Whereupon the two gentlemen saluted him.
Manly Frowde, suddenly seeing the salute,
awkwardly touched the battered brim of his
weather-beaten straw hat.

" Are you seriously going to inquire about
the house?" said Harry, as Frank showed
signs of walking up to Mr. Wemys's gate.

"Yes, I am ; I like the look of the place.
It looks quaint and original, and there is
some character to study here.   If the house

is neither too big nor too small, I have an
impulse to take it."

"You want to turn hermit, do you, after
seeing everything?   Be on your guard.
Hermits have been tempted in the loneliest
deserts."

" It will be a new sensation to be tempted
in a rustic corner like this.   We have seen
no daughters of Circe either at the village
inn or the village shop, have we?"

"Faith, I should think not," laughed
Rivers.

Mr. Wemys was a portly gentleman, who
received them with an air of pomposity.
He was one of those who put on a grand
dignified manner to hide some defect.
Such men are afraid to speak in a friendly
way to people of a lower class in case their
position should be mistaken.   If a labourer
ventured to remark to Mr. Wemys that it
was a fine day, he would reply as if he

patronized both the man and the weather.

"Ah," thought Frank Forncett, "I can see this man is a downright good fellow at heart, and I know what little defect he would hide by his manner. But he might be easy with me. Perhaps I can make him so before I have done with him."

After they had seen the house, which was a tolerably good one, with four or five acres of land attached to it, and had received all necessary information, Frank asked a few questions about the neighbourhood.

"Are you far from a station?" said Frank.

"Three and a half miles from the nearest, but that is a small one called Two Bridges, and we find Medenhithe, which is five miles away, the most convenient," said Mr. Wemys.

"Ah," exclaimed Frank, "we have just walked from there."

"Walked?" said Mr. Wemys in astonishment. "You must be very tired and hungry? Pray let me offer you something."

"Thank you, you are very kind; but a dozen miles is scarcely anything to me, and we got some bread and cheese at the inn. We intend making a tramp through the country, and took the train from town to Medenhithe this morning. We were so much struck with the view from the knoll, and the pretty appearance of the village, that we halted, and going to the village shop for postage-stamps and gossip, we heard that you wished to let your house. I have for some time been looking for a house that should be quite in the country, and yet not too far from London, and not near a railway; and I think this will exactly suit me. I should therefore like to take it at once to prevent anyone else from having it ; and if you will be kind enough to take my address, for I have not a card with me, we can afterwards settle all other matters."

Mr. Wemys was delighted to get the house off his hands so easily, for he had a long lease, and paid a fancy rent, and found it difficult to induce anyone to take it. When the matter was quite settled, the hospitable Mr. Wemys said :

" May I not persuade you to discontinue your perambulations for to-day, and to stay and dine with us ?   We dine at six."

"Thank you, I think we'd better tramp on."

" No, no ; let me find your young friend and talk to him, and then I am sure you will stay."

The " young friend " had, while looking over the stables, made acquaintance with young Wemys, a lively boy of twenty, who was waiting for his commission, and had to wait some time, as his name appeared a very long way down on the list at the examination. For all that, he was cut out for a soldier—had a manly look, plenty of energy, a sound constitution, and just the proper amount of pugnacity. His algebra might be shaky, but his nerves were not; and if he was dubious about the legs of that confounded isosceles triangle in the Pons Asinorum, he could use his own on a long tramp. He will probably make as good a figure as men much higher up the list. They were looking at some valuable little dogs that young Wemys was rearing, when Frank and Mr. Wemys joined them.

Harry Rivers was quite willing to stay to dine. " But we've no clothes with us," he said, " except some trifles in our knapsacks. Our clean linen is ordered to be left in readiness for us at certain inns where we have arranged to stop, and we hope not to put on a dress-coat for a month."

"Oh, never mind that," said young Wemys. "Look here, father," he said, turning to him, "you and I will dine as we are to keep these gentlemen company, and Ma and the girls will have to forgive us."

Mr. Wemys liked the dignity of the family kept up by everyone appearing dressed for dinner, and young Wemys, who was always a gentleman in any coat, used often to appear in morning dress. The old gentleman would put on his most dignified manner and inquire the reason, but his son would say, "Late this evening, sir—watch slow—very sorry—shan't occur again."

So it was arranged that they should stay to dine.

"I think, Mr. Wemys, we will sleep at the inn to-night, and start on our walk soon after daybreak to-morrow. Will you let your servant engage some bed-rooms for us?"

"I can hardly recommend you to go to the Pleiades, for Biggins, the landlord, is a most turbulent fellow and a great promoter of discord in the parish. Will you allow me to accommodate you?"

"Certainly not. You are very good, but I could not trouble you so far. I should like to go on very early in the morning, and would not take the liberty of disturbing your household. Is there another inn within reasonable distance?"

"There is one a few yards from my gate, which our friends have sometimes used when the house is full. If they can accommodate you, I think you might be comfortable," said Mr. Wemys.

"Thank you," said Frank; "that will suit us. You have no lack of inns."

"Unfortunately, we have thirteen public-houses in the district for a population of 850. So you may well understand that we are not free from drunkenness in these parts, though the peasantry generally are exceedingly well behaved on the whole—very well behaved "—said Mr. Wemys, relapsing into his patronising tone when he thought of "the lower orders." "The shopkeeper is, I think, a little given to gossip and mischief-making, but an excellent woman in her position—rather a rough tongue sometimes, and requires to be kept in her place —apt to forget when she is speaking to her superiors," he said loftily ; "it is that man Biggins who demoralizes the villagers. He encourages poachers and low characters, and anyone who has lost his place from dishonesty. I don't like to see a gentleman's servant hanging about at the Pleiades. I know he is doing no good there."

"Your parson is Mr. Bonfellow, I hear,"

said Frank. " I know something of his family."

"Estimable young man," said Mr. Wemys, "though sometimes a little lax in Church matters. A little more ritual would please me."

" And you have Mr. Manly Frowde here?" said Frank.

"Yes," said Mr. Wemys; " do you know him ?"

" Only his works," said Frank.

" I have a speaking acquaintance with him, but we don't visit," said Wemys, in a tone which clearly meant that Manly Frowde was somewhat beneath his notice. " He's a clever writer," he continued patronisingly.

" Are you much troubled with morning callers and dinner invitations ?" asked Forncett.

" No," said Wemys, who wished he had been more troubled in this way. " I do not find my neighbours very sociable; in fact, the dulness of the place makes me leave it. I do not care for society myself, but my young daughters must go out a little."

"The dulness will exactly suit me," said Frank. Frank Forncett could easily see why Mr. Wemys was not likely to be much visited.

There is no need to describe the dinner, which was well served and gaily eaten. Mrs. Wemys was a pleasant hostess, and the three young ladies agreeable enough, though they did not wound Harry Rivers's suscepti- ble heart. He thought little Kitty lively and pretty, but then she was only a child. They took leave early, and smoked a cigar with Wemys the younger, as he guided them to the Red House, a quiet, well-conducted inn, where they slept right soundly.

They were off again next morning at a

very early hour, meaning that night to sleep at the town where King Alfred was born, and to climb the White Horse Hill the day after; a good pull, with plenty of hill and dale, but they did not tire, being sound of wind and limb, and loving a long tramp in the open air. With the exception of some chops at East Ilsley (where mutton ought to be good considering its great sheep-fairs), they took nothing save the casual glass of ale till they reached the Bear, at Wantage.

"What a glorious day we have had!" said Harry Rivers, throwing himself into a chair, evidently built for the biggest farmer in the county. "What's to be had, waiter?"

"Steak and stout," said the functionary promptly.

"Hurrah!" exclaimed the exuberant Harry; "no oysters, of course? We're twenty thousand miles from anywhere. I say, Frank, has it occurred to you that you'll get nothing fit to eat at Copse Hill? The old boy's mutton-cutlets yesterday were mere fibre."

"I shall get everything from London," said Forncett; "Ralph does all that for me. I take no trouble."

"He's an invaluable fellow."

"Ay, he is. He's a clear brain and a active body, and the stillest tongue I ever knew."

Forncett went to bed that night well satisfied with what he had done so promptly. Always had he been given to neglecting the saying, that "second thoughts are best;" but for that propensity he might not at this moment have been a bachelor. He slept soundly after his long tramp; no vision of the night came to tell him that he had taken a step which would change the whole current of his life: no such presentiment reached him. The two pedestrians breakfasted together in the gayest humour, and tramped off early at five miles an hour in search of the Blowing Stone and the White Horse of Alfred.

CHAPTER IV.

THE NEW COMER.

Always a flutter of petticoats, always a whirlwind of
    chat,
  When a newcomer arrives in a village marvellous
    slow :
Tradesman hopes he has means, and may turn out a
    thundering flat ;
  Damsel hopes he has means, and may be a possible
    beau.

Cynicus de Re Rustica.

MR. WEMYS wished to leave The Birches as soon as possible, having heard of a house near town that would just suit him, while Frank Forncett was anxious to get into his new house. Therefore, about the middle of November several large vans arrived at The Birches, and the goods were moved in under the superintendence of Ralph.

This was quite a sensation for the village, a nine days' wonder, at least.

"Who is the new comer?" was every-one's question. Mrs. Biggins oracularly re-marked in the bar of the Pleiades that "whoever he was, he was no gentleman, as you might see by his dress."

"Any horses and carriages?" asked a gentleman's coachman.

"He won't have no horses and carriages," said Biggins, in a sneering tone; "he is something the same sort as that there fellow over there." (This was Biggins's usual way of mentioning Manly Frowde.) "He's a seedy chap, he is, and not worth much, I guess."

Biggins was a carrier as well as a publican and farmer, and kept large furniture vans, to which he gave names, One was the "Garibaldi," the name being painted in large yellow letters on a red ground on the side of the van. Biggins had an idea somewhere in his stolid old head that Garibaldi was a great man, though if you had asked him what he knew about him, he would have been puzzled to say.

"What's old Garry doing now?" he would often say to anyone who he thought read the papers and knew what was going on in the world.

But he has lately found another hero in the Tichborne claimant, and relates with pride how he has been considered by some people to be like "that unhappy nobleman in Dartmoor." If he should set up a new furniture van he will no doubt name it after his new hero. He seems to have a misty notion that when "old Garry" comes over here, everything will be made right, and

Roger will get his own again. Now, if Ralph had employed Biggins to bring the furniture and had not objected to paying what Biggins would call "handsome and like a real gentleman," Frank Forncett would have been heralded by a flourish of trumpets from the frequenters of the Pleiades at least.

"They say there's not much to be expected from the new gentleman," said one of the good wives of the village, at Miss Tattleton's, as she was carefully laying out her small weekly allowance, on a Saturday afternoon, in provisions for the following week.

"Who told you so?" said Miss Tattleton, rather sharply, weighing out a quarter of a pound of tea, which was supposed to be sufficient to serve a family of six for a week.

"My husband says as how he heard Mrs. Biggins say so."

"And what does she know about it?" said Miss Tattleton. "You wait till you see," she said, with a significant nod, and she pushed the tea tightly down in the paper as she packed it to make room for an extra handful, which she put in before tying it up, and handed it with a look as much as to say, "I speak sharp, but I give you an ounce of tea to make up."

This was her usual way of treating poor customers, and may perhaps account for the fact that she has not yet made her fortune.

Among the many inquiries at Miss Tattleton's about the new comer, was Mrs. Lovelace, who liked a bit of gossip dearly. She had been a very handsome woman, and was trying to grow old gracefully, as Madame de Staël puts it, but did not succeed. She came mincing into the shop, dressed in a style that would have been delightful in a girl of eighteen, but which scarcely suited her maturity.

"Well, Miss Tattleton," she said, "1 hear that somebody has taken Mr. Wemys's house. I hope he is some one on whom county families can call; so many doubtful characters come into this neighbourhood, and Captain Lovelace, as you know, is very particular."

"Yes, ma'am, we know the Captain is quite right to be particular. I think the gentleman who is coming to The Birches is very pleasant, but not quite the sort that you and the Captain would like. He is, 1 think, more like my neighbour opposite," said Miss Tattleton, pointing to Mr. Manly Frowde's house.

"Oh! do you think he is only an author?" said Mrs. Lovelace, looking very much disappointed. "That would be a great loss to county society; we don't want any more of those troublesome authors about. We have been hoping we should get a nice family here."

"I wouldn't say he was an author," said Miss Tattleton; "though I have heard that there are large chestfuls of books come down with the luggage."

"I can't think why these authors dress so badly," said Mrs. Lovelace, "unless it is that they are so very poor. What a guy that poor Mrs. Manly Frowde makes of herself. I really quite pity the poor creature, though I don't suppose she knows how bad she looks."

"At any rate, she always looks happy, and I am sure you and the Captain set a good example in dressing," said Miss Tattleton, looking admiringly at Mrs. Lovelace's rich dress; "and we can't all be good-looking," she said archly.

Mrs. Lovelace tossed her head coquettishly, delighted with the compliment, and forgetting that the pretty little coquettish movements, which are so sweet in a girl, are contemptible in an elderly woman. She was one of those weak women who are completely conquered by a little flattery.

It is a brave sight to see an old man or woman bearing the weight of age cheerfully. Old age is too often made ugly. Young people, instead of reverencing their elders, laugh at them, or are frightened of them; and how common it is to hear young people say that they hope they may never grow old! But when, as sometimes happens, the experience of age is combined with the freshness of youth, it is a glorious sight, enough to make one wish to grow old.

Unfortunately, some people try to keep the freshness of youth by painting and adorning the body instead of adorning the mind, and such can only be melancholy objects. The true way to render age vigorous is to prolong the youth of the mind.

By the end of November The Birches was in perfect order, ready for its new master. The indefatigable Ralph had engaged a couple of maid servants and a groom, who were all paid very high wages, on the understanding that they would be dismissed at a moment's notice, and forfeit a month's wages, if they were known to gossip of their master's affairs. It had been impossible to get any information from Ralph, but it was quite expected that the other servants would talk. When it was found that they were silent, the verdict in the village was that the new gentleman was somebody mysterious, Biggins suggesting that he had no doubt done something he was ashamed of, or he wouldn't keep his affairs so dark.

" And I don't think much of that precious

man of his," said Biggins, " a ordering everybody about as if his master was a lord, and
never giving a civil word to anybody. If
he and his master thinks they're going to
keep their affairs to themselves they're a
precious lot mistaken, for the old cat over
there 'll soon find out all about 'em, and if
she don't, I will, blessed if I don't;" and he
brought down his hand with a mighty thump
on the table. Biggins's oaths—and he used
one on almost every occasion—need not be
repeated. They were rather monotonous,
consisting chiefly of a sanguinary adjective
and a condemnatory allusion to the eyes.

It is calculated that a first-class English
orator will use about ten thousand words, and
an English peasant three hundred. Compul-
sory education being unheard of at Copse
Hill, the vocabulary of the labourers is represented by about three hundred words.
So the oaths are necessarily not much

varied, and Biggins's fine monotony is closely imitated by his admirers, who are numerous. The boy of ten, who hears the huge land-lord's sonorous execration, passes it on an hour or two later to his comrade of eight. Miss Tattleton's admirably ironical laudation of the village showed very much what it was not. This is the sort of thing you find in the country where the parson is powerless for good, where the education is inferior, where country gentlemen neglect their duty to their dependents.

Before Frank Forncett comes to the vil-lage which is athirst for the mysterious stranger, the hero of this story must appear, else the reader may take the new tenant of The Birches for the hero, which he is not by any means. He may play Mercutio to the hero's Romeo, or Horatio to his Hamlet, who knows? One thing is certain, that had not Frank Forncett taken with such fatality of promptitude Wemys's house, he would never have had revealed to him the great mistake of his earlier life—would never have come face to face with his boyish self, and wondered what a fool he had been. We never know what trivial incident may change for us the aspect of the world.

CHAPTER V.

THE HERO AT HOME.

I want a hero—an uncommon want.
BYRON.

THE parish of Ashton Minima, in the county of Oakshire, had, at the census of 1871, twelve inhabitants.   At the census of 1861, it possessed thirteen inhabitants. The wife of the keeper of the turnpike-gate died somewhere between those two dates, and nothing had occurred to increase the population.   The parish is a sinecure rectory, without a church; and the only houses beside that at the toll-bar are the rectory, which contained seven inhabitants, and a small public-house, the Waggon and Horses, which contained four. Yet is it a large parish as to acreage; but landowners and farmers live beyond its boundaries, for it is almost all heath and moorland, good for the partridge, and not altogether bad for the sheep.

The Reverend Marston Sebright, sinecure Rector of Ashton Minima, was a man doubly, perhaps trebly, disappointed. His father was that famous Bishop Sebright who invented a new reading of the damnatory clauses of the Creed erroneously ascribed to Athanasius. Marston Sebright, his only son, who took high honours at the university, and might have risen to the highest rank in the ecclesiastical hierarchy, had unhappily a constitutional affliction which incapacitated him—he had a chronic asthma, which compelled him to speak in a whisper. Such being the case, he could never hope to wear lawn sleeves in the House of Lords, a position which episcopal fatherhood and remarkable talent might well have attained for him. A sinecure rectory suited him well: he married, had one son, and devoted himself to editing classical authors. He felt within him the power to teach Christianity to the people with no common influence, but physical inability rendered that power useless.

His second disappointment was in his wife, one of the most charming creatures in the world, who made him thoroughly comfortable, and who distinctly declined to be discontented, or to sympathize with his discontent. Marston Sebright was intensely ambitious, and saw all the higher levels of ambition placed beyond his reach! His wife had no ambition, and wanted him to be happy with her in their strangely solitary home. He could not; he felt like a caged eagle. He longed to find utterance for his ideas in the oratoric form. He would wander over the moorland for hours trying to articulate aloud, and his voice would be merely a whisper.

Marston Sebright's third disappointment was his son—our hero. Jack Sebright (nobody had ever been known to call him John) was simply the happiest young fellow on this earth's surface. He had never had a headache or a toothache; he possessed a strength of the Hercules type; at the same time, without being a genius, or even a clever fellow, he managed to graduate in honours at Cambridge, after being captain of the boats at Eton. He got among the wranglers, not by real mathematical science, but by the physical strength which enabled him to cram anything. It was memory, the physical faculty, that set him above many men of greater intellectual

power than himself. If we look at our
statesmen, we find that brain can only come
to the front when there is backbone to help
it. The power which made Jack Sebright
seventh wrangler made him the fastest
round-hand bowler of his time. He dismissed mathematics from his memory when
he left college. He did not dismiss cricket.

Now the Reverend Marston Sebright
wanted this boy, the great Bishop Sebright's
grandson, endowed with physical powers
which he, unhappily, had missed, to enter
the Church and keep up the hereditary
ecclesiastical renown. The youngster did
not seem to see it. His kind mother, a
quiet creature, whose sole desire was to
make father and son happy, did what she
could to persuade him. That rebellious
backbone of his militated against it; he'd
have liked to be a soldier or a sailor rather
—perhaps even a tinker or a tailor. He

had doubts—real honest conscientious doubts—of his fitness to undertake a cure of souls. Many people do undertake it with far less fitness than Jack Sebright.

His father sent him abroad to have a look at the world when he found him in this impracticable mood. Marston Sebright had great faith in the influence of time and change. He remembered how fiercely he had rebelled against his own great disappointment, and now he was content, though perhaps not quite happy, when the great critical journals told him he was the best classical scholar in England. That had not been his ambition—he had longed to be a great preacher. Vain to murmur: each soldier of God must take his allotted place in the great army.

Jack Sebright obeyed his father's behest, and zig-zagged through Europe. Travel suited that untirable backbone of his. He was quite ready to scale the Andes, or row round the world in a canoe. His hidden power wanted development, and he had not yet decided in what way it should be exercised. His father thought he would make a capital parson, but this is a world in which people are extremely inclined to differ from their fathers—and to be very savage when their sons differ from them.

After wandering in many directions, he came to Venice. It was evening on the Piazza di S. Marco. The mighty tower which maddened the author of *The Stones of Venice* threw its long shapely shadow across the noble square. Jack Sebright heard an English voice asking some casual question. He saw in the moonlight a tall broad-shouldered fellow, who was manifestly English. With the natural freemasonry of Englishmen he addressed him, and in a few minutes they were sitting together on chairs in the moonlight, while an active waiter brought refreshment, and they watched some girls dancing in the distance.

"A magic scene this," said Manly Frowde, for it was he whom Sebright had accosted. "My wife and I must be off to-morrow, for there is work awaiting me in England. You take your time, I suppose?"

"I came to-day, and want to see this wonderful city."

"You are right. Here is Antonio Quadri's guide-book, which I have done with. It was published in 1827, but is curiously faithful to the old churches and palaces—so little are they changed. But there's a magic of poetry about Venice: you might meet Shylock on the Rialto, and think of little locked-up Jessica, resolved to run away. Then there's Schiller's seer of ghosts, and Voltaire's dinner of the six dethroned kings. And can't you imagine Byron and Shelley fluttering pieces of paper from their window for the innumerable pigeons to fly after? Poets are such fools, you see, and Shelley has been known to turn a five-pound note into a paper boat and float it away upon a pond."

"I should like to meet you when I get back to England," said Sebright, with no very definite connexion.

"Easy enough," replied the other; "I've a little place at Copse Hill in Oakshire, a few miles from Two Bridges, and my wife is always pleased to receive a visitor who isn't a prig."

"I hope I'm not that," said Sebright, laughing in a tone that startled the piazza. "I'm so glad to hear you live near my father's place. It's Ashton Minima; he's parson there, without a church; and he wants me to be parson too, and I don't half like it."

" A sinecure rectory," said Frowde. " You are about a dozen miles from me. Can you find your way over ?"

" I've been there before. There's no mistaking the two clumps of trees at the top of the beautiful hill, or the stolid stout landlord at the bottom. I'll come over, if I may."

" Better come now and ask my wife," said Frowde. " She likes enthusiastic young fellows, and perhaps she can give you better advice than I can about entering the Church. My opinion is that the men who have conscientious scruples against taking orders are the very men who should do it and be of use. I have rather a weakness for a fellow with a conscience. The sort of parson I detest is the man who stands by his office, does innumerable silly things, and says they must be right, because he was divinely ordained."

Jack Sebright went right willingly to Frowde's hotel, and was introduced to Mrs. Frowde ;—a lady made of flesh and blood, with a soft white style of dress in lace and frill that suited her Persephone form, with sunlit brown hair leaving with a perfect curve the broad forehead that indicates power and love. She saw through this young fellow at once, and liked him ; and not long was it before, over a light Venetian supper, they were frankly discussing this boy's prospects.

"You see," he said ruefully, but with a glass of light wine ready to wash down his trouble, "my father says that because his father was a bishop, I ought to be. Now do you agree with that?"

"It may be logical," said Frowde, "but it does not seem to work. One of my grandfathers was a schoolmaster and the other a soldier; and I am neither, but a poor scribbler."

"I wish I could write," said Sebright.

"Try," said Frowde. "It is not, except in accidental cases, a lucrative occupation, but I suppose it is the most gratifying to the human mind. 1 write for filthy lucre, though I would write willingly for fame, if in these days fame could be obtained by the eagle's flight—straight sunward. It cannot: and the only man who in these times can live by writing is the man who does not care what he writes, or the man who has money enough to pay for the issue of his work."

"I should like to break through the vile system," said Sebright, broadening his stalwart shoulders.

"Come and see us when you return," said Mrs. Frowde, smiling at his fine boyish enthusiasm. "We'll talk over parsons and publishers after dinner. We can give you a bed in a homely way."

"I'd sleep on the roof rather than not come," said Jack Sebright.

CHAPTER VI.

THE HEROINE BY THE SEA.

ALOUETTE.—I like the sea, Prince.

RAFAEL.—Yes, the flying yacht, you know.

With topmost royals, making timber perilous,
And a gay wind to race with!

ALOUETTE.—Ah, but plunge in it!

Down in the depths cool your hot eyes
with emerald

Wave made for mermaids! Fathom the
abysses where

Strange creatures dwell—a world unknown, unknowable—

Perhaps a race more great than men can
ever be!

The Comedy of Dreams.

"MR., MRS., AND MISS TEMPLE."
Thus ran the announcement in the
Visitor's Guide to the pleasant South Devon

village of Dawlish—beautiful still, though the inexorable Brunel spoilt it by running the railway right across the estuary of its delightful little river, which sparkles between green lawns to the sea. He could not spoil the crescent of sand, the tall red cliffs, the silver-sounding midnight moaning sea. The stern old King of Ocean, whom Homer has named the Shaker of Earth, seems calmer along that sinuous sweep of Devon. He seldom rages into hurricane. He comes whispering musically up the shore, and kisses the dainty feet of pretty girls.

This is a very pretty girl who trips daintily along the sands right early in the autumn morning. She is going to the machines. She is in the most delicate costume for a bather; her amber hair is loose over her shoulders; her eyes are almost too demurely hidden by dark-lashed lids. She sees no one as she hurries across to her bathing-machine, dressed in a style that seems rather to suit Trouville or Deauville than quiet little Dawlish. Old Captain Radmore, who always turns out in the morning to look at vessels in the offing, but whose glass sometimes sweeps the sands when there are women about, has on this occasion his attention divided. He sees a mighty monster of the deep steaming down Channel, and says to himself,

"That's the *Thunderbolt*. She'll go down, with all on board, and then perhaps they'll hang the Lords of the Admiralty."

Yet he also sees this pretty coquette tripping down to the sea, and soliloquizes thus:

"By Jove! a new arrival. A tidy saucy little craft. Wonder who she is."

He watched her through his glass. Just before she reached the little row of bathing-machines, a tall gentleman passed her pretty close. Each gave a perceptible start, but no greeting occurred between them.

The Captain shut his telescope with a snap.

"Some romance there," he thought. "I should like to find it out."

O energetic fellow-creature, were it not better to create a romance of thy own than to espy and eavesdrop some other human being's romance? Romance is a good thing; would there were more of it in the world. It is the middle space between high poetry and dull prose. Few men can be poets, fewer women; but all men or women who are not governed by evil influences—by fashion or fanaticism, by vanity, the love of slander, and other meannesses of the lower intellect—can enter and enjoy the glorious demesnes of romance, so exquisitely described by Coleridge in his *Garden of Boccaccio* :—

> I wander through the Eden of thy hand,
> Praise the green arches, on the fountain clear
> See fragment shadows of the crossing deer;
> And with that serviceable nymph I stoop
> The crystal from its restless pool to scoop.
> I see no longer! I myself am there,
> Sit on the ground-sward, and the banquet share.

That banquet is open to all who ask for the key of the garden. But who asks? Most men pass contemptuously by, on their way to one of the many temples of Mammon.

Captain Radmore speculated, of course wide of the mark. The vagaries of a big ironclad, built to reach the bottom of the sea, were more in his way than those of a young lady with hair of the latest dye, and a costume for the seaside fresh from Paris. As to that young lady, she went on to her morning bath, looking neither to the right nor the left, and assuming a delightful un-consciousness.

Not so the gentleman she had met, and

who had recognized her.   A shudder passed through him.   A tall calm quiet man, whose talk was brief but choice, who had seen many lands and many events, who held that difficulties were made to be overcome, and troubles made to be forgotten.   An excellent creed: but why should a forgotten trouble turn up here at quiet red-sanded Dawlish, with a new colour in her hair but the same wicked look in her eyes?   He felt it hard upon him.   He walked rapidly home to his lodgings, which were in a large house facing the sea, close to the red cliff which shuts out the pretty village from all things else save illimitable water.

Ascending to the first floor, he met a lady, tall and nobly developed, with much dark hair and very soft grey eyes, and kissed her lips.

" Where is the child ?" he asked.

" Gone for a bath.   You don't look well,

William. Take a glass of hock before you breakfast."

"Thanks, Leonora," he said. "Where is Kate gone to bathe? Away to the left?"

He took a field-glass, and looked along the line of ugly machines that defaced the full curve of the little bay.

"To the left, I think she goes; but why do you ask?"

" Well, I have just met Flora."

" Again?"

"Yes, she seems to haunt us. I don't want to curtail my darling's liberty, but I dread what harm might be done if Flora met her."

"She has too much sense," said Leonora decisively. "She knows the truth both from you and me, and she is a girl of very clear intellect. I don't fear her, William; you need not."

" Kate is not easily shaken in her convictions," answered Mr. Temple; "but you must remember how curiously plausible and persuasive Flora is. Her way of following us is significant of some ridiculous purpose; we saw her in Paris, we saw her at Brighton, we saw her in such an out-of-the-way place as Clevedon. Now, I don't believe she can do any harm, but I hate annoyance; and I wish we could find a house inland that would suit us. Flora would not follow us into a quiet village. She must have her amusement. She is a mere butterfly, that has singed her wings. I am simply sorry for her; I do the best I can for her; but I am not able to bear these constant persecutions. We must go elsewhere. I wish we could find the sort of place we want."

"Oh, so do I !" said the lady. "Kate might find it dull; but, if you take her to town now and then, and give her a course of opera and theatre, you'll keep her brain alive. I am proud of Kate. She enjoys life wisely. She is very inquisitive and very speculative, and enthusiastic when she finds sure ground for enthusiasm."

" Your character is laconic. Pray explain, Leonora."

"Well, I'll put a special question. Suppose she met Flora? She would try to find out all about her. On what little she could gain from her conversation she would base her own opinion. Then she would, with that suppressed enthusiasm of hers, love or hate her intensely."

" And which do you think ?"

" Hate."

"Horrible thought !" said Temple, pressing his hands to his forehead.

" Yes, dear William," said Leonora ; " but would not love be far more horrible ?"

At this moment the waiter entered with letters.

"Now, perhaps," said the lady, "we shall find your house-agent has heard of some place to suit us. Shall I look through the letters?"

"Do, darling," he said. "That meeting with Flora has disgusted me. You understand my feelings; no one else does."

She kissed him on the forehead as he lay back in his chair, saying,

"It would be strange indeed if I did not understand them. We have suffered alike; but we have our love left, an undying love."

"We have, indeed," he said. "And we have our dear Kate to bring forward quietly, and to save her, if we can, from the troubles we have endured."

She opened several letters, none of which seemed of much consequence. At last she came upon one from the house-agent, who informed them that he thought he had found exactly the thing they wanted—large rooms, ten acres of ground, three and a half miles from the station of Two Bridges, which is merely a small one with few trains in the day; situated in a small village, and some distance from the road; the neighbourhood very quiet.

"That sounds well," said Mr. Temple; "but we have looked at so many, and been disappointed. Where is it?"

"The house is called Winterslow, and is in the village of Copse Hill, in Oakshire."

"Well, we had better look at it, Leonora; for we must make some effort to avoid these disagreeable meetings. I wish it were further from a station; but it is conveniently near London. I know something of the neighbourhood, though I do not remember that I was ever in Copse Hill. I suppose it cannot be far from the Thames, and that would suit Kate and the dogs. Let us, at any rate, leave here to-day or to-morrow, and go to town; and then we can run down and look at the place."

"I shall be delighted," said Leonora, "to get to some quiet nook where I can forget my trouble; and I long to begin again my favourite occupation of gardening. But I am afraid it will be a dull life for poor Kate."

"Nonsense, Leonora; I'll take care that neither you nor Kate shall be dull."

"Was I ever dull with you, William?" she said, taking both his hands in hers.

"I hope not," he said, with a loving smile. "You are the bravest woman in the world, my Leonora."

At this moment in comes, or rather rushes, Kate Temple. She is sea-drenched. A gay girl of eighteen, not quite so tall as Leonora, she is far more excitable. She cries out—

"Oh, papa, mamma! I have had quite an adventure. When I came out of the machine a lady spoke to me. So lovely, with long yellow hair, eyes blue as sapphires, and such a pretty pleasing soft way. I should not call her honest, I think," said the outspoken girl.

Mr. Temple shuddered. Those words, too true, were terrible to him from those lips.

"And what did she say?" asked Leonora.

"She talked as if she were mad," replied Kate Temple. "I think she must be mad, mamma. She said first, 'Are you Miss Temple?' and of course I said I was. Then she said that I should be sure to come to a bad end, for the Temples always did."

Mr. Temple laughed at his pretty daughter.

"Some half-crazed creature, Kate, depend on it. You won't be troubled with her again, for I think of going to London to-morrow, and I have just heard of a house in the country which may perhaps suit us. We have been wandering so long that a little quietude will be pleasant."

" It will indeed, papa," said Kate, always ready for a new movement.

So telegrams were sent to hotels, and luggage packed rapidly, for when Mr. Temple decided to move his servants had to move also. The quietest man in Europe, he always had his way in such matters. Pretty Kate was delighted at the move, but she came down rather out of form to catch the early train. She had dreamt a strange dream of the lady she saw on Dawlish sands : and there was in her mind a troubling thought—" Can it be ? But no : it could not, for she looked so very young."

CHAPTER VII.

A SINGED BUTTERFLY.

Θεοὶ ῥεῖα ζώοντες.—*Odyssey*, v. 122.

THE gods of old Greece were neither moral nor immoral, but profoundly indifferent to ethical questions. This, doubtless, was the natural tendency of the Greek mind in its earlier state. The Heroic Age, as described by Homer, is one in which no idea of the Ten Commandments ever entered into the mind of man, still less into the mind of any divinity. The schoolboy—if there be such a phenomenon who studies his Lemprière or Smith intelli-

gently, must be rather amazed at the say-
ings and doings of certain gods and heroes,
goddesses and heroines. There is not an
immaculate character in the whole my-
thology. Yet the work of Greece in the
world was a work unparalleled, and its
poetic creations were without the faintest
rivalry till one William Shakespeare arose.

"The gods live at their ease," says
Calypso, in the *Odyssey*; "and there are
men, and indeed women, who, though not
god-like in much else, have that touch of
Greek divinity. Such a man is Arundel
Lifton, who is just now lounging along the
West Pier at Brighton. Straight as an
arrow, dressed to perfection, with hair and
moustache untouched by the hand of time,
no one would guess him to be half-a-century
old. He carefully forgets it himself. He
is in the prime of life, and why should he
count years? Born to a vast fortune in

Cornish mines, educated at Eton and Christ-
church, left by the early death of his father
to do just as he pleased, he had lived a life of
calculative voluptuousness. He believed in
one god—and that god was himself. He
resolved to have as much pleasure as possible, with as little pain. He never drank or
smoked to excess; he never sat up im-
moderately late; he never gambled or
betted; and—which amazed his acquaintances (he had no friends) more than anything
—he never travelled by rail. He had tried it
once, and it had bored him and fretted him,
and next day he read of an awful railway
accident: so he kept to the road thereafter.
There was never the slightest need for him
to be in a hurry; he was accustomed to send
horses forward on any long journey. " You
can stop where you like in your own
carriage," he used to say; " in a train you
are at the mercy of a sooty engine-driver.

I have one principle throughout life—and that is, to be my own master."

He carried out this principle to the utmost. He married, in the bloom of her delicious youth, one of the sweetest girls in the world, and then deserted her in a way most shameful. He was quite ready to make her a large allowance: she, being a lady pure and simple, declined to accept a farthing from him, and lived on her own small fortune. Happily, they had no child. Then he took his own way. He liked adventure that was spiced by wickedness. He paid like a prince for his amusements. Hitherto, princely payment had, strange to say, taken him safely through his cool evil career; he had not met anyone with hot blood, or cudgel or rapier, to punish him as he deserved. He had a charmed luck, probably.

We first behold him on the West Pier.

He has been a day or two at the Old Ship
Hotel, which comfortable hostelry has long
been used to his habits, and where certain
quiet rooms are always reserved for him.
Arundel Lifton likes 'not to be disturbed.
He hates a scene above all things. He does
not like the patrician pretentiousness of the
Bedford, or the noisy splendour of the
Grand. He is (and it is one of his few
good points) as keen a judge of wine as any
man in Europe. Wisely said the Arab
sage, "To choose thy caravanserai, taste its
forbidden liquor."

Arundel Lifton dined in his private room
that night on mutton and game, with a
bottle of choice Lafitte. He was an epicure
on principle, and studied the composition of
every meal he ate. To-night there is a ball
at the Grand Hotel, and he thinks he will
look in. Those hotel balls are rather an
American idea, but they seem to go well in

Brighton—where indeed most things do go well. So Mr. Lifton, an hour or so after dinner, dressed indolently. He never employed a valet. "Such a bore to tell the fellow what to do—less trouble to do it yourself:" thus said Mr. Lifton. He slowly got himself into evening dress by his bed-room fire, and then said to himself,

"By Jove! What an exertion! I think I may allow myself a glass of Chartreuse."

A brougham was waiting. He was at the Grand Hotel in two minutes. It was now about eleven. He entered without much expectation of amusement, but found a gay and vivid scene. The hall and corridors were steeped in light. Doubtless the company was mixed (for Brighton is the modern Corinth), but the dress-coats and the toilettes were superb, and what more can you want? Homer mentions a people who cared for very little except yachting, banqueting, music, dances, clean linen, baths, and beds. Whoso doubts this statement, let him read the eighth book of the *Odyssey*. Humanity changes little.

Arundel Lifton, the most distinguished man there, with an air of mystery about him, an air of haughtiness, leans against a column and looks round. The M.C. of the night proposes introduction to a partner, but he declines in so quietly lofty a way that the M.C. thinks him a royal personage incognito. As a fact, he is faultless. He has so graceful a figure that any tailor would gladly dress him for nothing. But Arundel Lifton laughs at tailors, invents his own coats, and pays ready money. He does not aim to set the fashion, like Brummel, George IV., and Count D'Orsay : for he is a hand-some man of sufficient inches and of stal-wart chest, and to follow his method of dress the puny striplings of fashion would have to grow.

He looked on philosophically. Presently he caught a glimpse of a lady in a waltz. She had amber hair; she was dressed so that the light fabric showed the beauty of her shoulders, the soft curve of her breasts; she was deliciously piquant and pretty. She looked a girl—she had looked a girl a few weeks ago at Dawlish; but she was quite as capable of maintaining the appearance of youth as Arundel Lifton himself.

"Flora, by Jove!" he said to himself. "I caught her eye. What's the best thing? By Jove! I'll go and talk to her. We can't have a row in a ball-room."

So he took the bull by the horns, and walked up to her, somewhat to her surprise.

" You look charming to-night, Flora," he said.

" I feel miserable."

" There is no need. Come, let me take

you to have some supper; the fowls will be all drumsticks if we don't make haste. These Brighton folk, and especially the American visitors, have an infinite affection for liver wings."

"I wish I could cry a little," she said, "and nobody saw me. Oh! how I wish I could pray! You have made me wicked, Arundel: you will have to bear some of my punishment."

"You silly child! Come along, and we'll get some lobster salad and Chablis. The beggars generally keep something for me in these places, because I always give them something."

"How much you think about money, Arundel!"

"Of course I do. It's the lucifer match of the fire of life. It has bought me many things. It bought *you*, you hussy."

It was hard for Flora to restrain tears at

such insult, but the public were around her, and she kept calm.

"Arundel," she said, in a low whisper, "if you must speak to me like this, we had better not meet again. You have caused me unendurable misery, and now you treat me in this scandalous way. I could have forgiven you if you had been a gentleman, Arundel. Good night."

She flung away hotly, and left Mr. Lifton to his own reflections, which were quite untroubled.

CHAPTER VIII.

MRS. SELFE AT WINTERSLOW.

After her health we asked,
  Our care and regard to evince :
We have made the very same speeches
  To many an old cat since.
          HEINE (Mrs. Browning's translation).

IT was some two or three weeks after Mr. Forncett's first visit to Copse Hill with his friend, Harry Rivers, that Mr. Temple arrived with his daughter at Medenhithe station, whence they drove to Winterslow. Here they were most courteously received by Mrs. Selfe—a handsome, sweet-looking old lady, with a peculiar softness about her. She had a quantity of very white hair, a soft, pale complexion, and a sweet low voice; these, with her pretty dress of grey silk and white lace, made such a picture that Kate felt quite enthusiastic.

Mr. Temple found, after a little conversation, that Mrs. Selfe was inclined to change her mind, and did not wish to let her house —at least, for that winter. She was profuse in apologies for having given him so much trouble, but she had only made her decision on the previous day.

"This is a pretty neighbourhood," said Mr. Temple, "and I am sorry, for my own sake, that you have decided not to leave. Do you know if there is any other house to let?"

"The opposite neighbour is going away; but I understand that his house has just been taken by a bachelor. I forget the gentleman's name."

If the gentleman's name had been mentioned, it would no doubt have prevented the Temples from wishing to live at Copse Hill.

"Well, if you should again change your mind—and you know we allow ladies to do so as often as they like—you will perhaps be kind enough to let me know through your agents, and give me the first chance," said Mr. Temple, who had set his heart on the place, as it exactly suited him.

"Certainly," said Mrs. Selfe; "you may depend on me. And now let me offer you a little luncheon after your journey," she said, in the sweetest manner.

Mr. Temple looked at his daughter, and saw that it would please her, so accepted Mrs. Selfe's hospitality.

Mrs. Selfe was an intellectual woman, in one sense of the word. She liked "plain living and high thinking." Her "living" was plain enough; but whether her "thinking " had much height or depth is doubtful. However, she despised so gross and sensual a thing as feeding, and would have preferred to live in a world where it was not necessary. There was one weakness she acknowledged—she liked fruit; but she considered that taste as no more sensual than liking flowers for their sweet smell or pretty look.

It is rather difficult to draw a line in these matters. If one person has no taste for food, is he to condemn another who has? And if one person finds that it suits his constitution to be a teetotaller, is he to condemn another who finds that a glass of wine suits him?

Mrs. Selfe was a teetotaller, and almost a vegetarian, and she looked down with contempt on people who required more food than herself. Therefore the lunch offered to Mr. Temple and his daughter was somewhat frugal; indeed, Kate, with her healthy appetite, and after a five miles drive on a fresh October morning, with the west wind in her face, could have eaten everything on the table.

Mrs. Selfe was a democrat and Unitarian, and dabbled in a little science and free-thinking; so the conversation at lunch took a scientific turn, and Kate wondered why such a sweet-looking old lady should care to use such long words and talk so learned-ly. Then Garibaldi was mentioned, for his portrait hung on the wall; and it was dis-covered that Mrs. Selfe was an enthusiastic disciple of Garibaldi, though she did not seem to understand much about the free-dom of Italy—but her son had been killed in fighting under Garibaldi.

"Oh, how sad!" exclaimed Kate; "and have you any more children?"

"Two others," she said, as if unwilling to answer.

"And are they girls, or boys?" said Kate, without noticing the old lady's confusion.

" I have two daughters," she said, rather stiffly.

" Kate, dear," said Mr. Temple, seeing there was something that annoyed Mrs. Selfe in this question, " won't you eat one of those beautiful apples ? Does your orchard produce these ?" he said, turning to Mrs. Selfe to prevent Kate from continuing her catechism.

" Yes," she answered; "I have some very fine sorts, and a great many more than I can consume or want for my friends. I am obliged to sell some."

After lunch they went to see a vine in the greenhouse which Mrs. Selfe had grown from a cutting taken from Garibaldi's vine in Caprera, the bunches of which she distributed among her friends as something sacred.

They then took their leave, with a renewed promise that Mr. Temple should be informed if Mrs. Selfe should again change her mind.

"Oh, papa!" said Kate, when they were alone, "what a charming old lady! But, do you know, she reminds me of a beautiful big white cat; and when she talks in that soft voice it is just like a cat purring. When I first saw her I felt just as if I had seen a beautiful cat that I wanted to stroke.   And I really think, papa, she is like a cat in another way, for I can fancy that if you stroked her the wrong way she would ruffle up her fur, and stick up her back, and dart fire from her eyes and hiss at you."

"I think, Kate, you were very nearly rubbing her back the wrong way when you were so inquisitive about her children."

"Oh, yes, papa! Did you notice how stiff she was? Oh! I did so long to know about her daughters. I am sure there is something mysterious."

As these daughters will appear in our history, we will for the present leave Kate and her father, and give some little history of Mrs. Selfe and her family, for which purpose we will commence a new chapter.

CHAPTER IX.

MATERNAL AFFECTION.

"In reality, though, she hated her own son: of which, however monstrous it appears, I am assured she is not a singular instance."—FIELDING.

THE motto of this chapter is taken from *Tom Jones*, and applies excellent well to Mrs. Selfe, inasmuch as she hated her own daughters—at least it is to be presumed so from her treatment of them. Having been left a widow with a comfortable fortune while the girls were young, she brought them up according to her own fancy, and exercised the greatest tyranny over them. Her son, who was some years older than his sisters, disliking the restraint of home, so soon as he could realise the legacy left him by his father, went to Australia. Then his mother found out that she loved him, and would have given anything to bring him back; but it was too late. He came back, only to go away again after any wild adventure. He was eventually killed while fighting with Garibaldi, and was then canonised by his mother.

The daughters, Diana and Claudia, unfortunately could not run away, though they often longed to do so. They were jealously guarded from companions of their own age; with what object it is difficult to understand. But, as they grew up, they made friends with some of their mother's visitors, and enlisted their sympathies. Then Mrs. Selfe would leave her house and go into a new neighbourhood. She had tried three different neighbourhoods in this way, when

she finally settled at Copse Hill, thinking,
no doubt, that in such a dull place Diana
and Claudia would have little chance of
making acquaintances. One indulgence she
allowed them—namely, riding. This they
owed to their father, who had always wished
that they should be good riders, and had
taught them himself. When they came
to Copse Hill they were informed that they
could no longer have the use of the horses
and groom.

Mrs. Selfe and the Frowdes soon formed
a pleasant neighbourly acquaintance. Books
and papers were exchanged, as were also
gardening and knitting experiences, between
Mrs. Selfe and Mrs. Frowde. Diana and
Claudia were away when this acquaintance
commenced, and when they came home
Mrs. Frowde observed that Mrs. Selfe was
unwilling that they should see her when she
called. Also Mrs. Selfe seemed uncomfort-

able when in their presence. One day, out walking, Claudia met the Frowdes, and said:

"Oh, Mrs. Frowde, do please lend me some books. I am so dull at home, for my sister is away, and the house is so silent. The only cheerful sound I ever hear is Mr. Frowde's laugh from your garden."

"We've plenty of books," said Mrs. Frowde, "come and choose for yourself, and pray do come in whenever you like."

This led to many visits from Diana and Claudia, and also to an entire breaking off of the acquaintance between the Frowdes and Mrs. Selfe.

Mrs. Selfe seems to find it impossible to be friendly with anyone who likes her daughters.

Diana and Claudia found their visits to the Cottage so pleasant that they spent a great deal of time there. Their mother, annoyed at seeing them happy, forbade them ever to visit the Frowdes again. They respectfully declined to obey this order, as they were old enough to choose their own friends. Then they should be turned out of their home, their mother said. They reminded her that she was bound to provide for them by their father's will, but, on suitable provision being made, they were quite ready to leave home if their mother wished it. She was not inclined to make any provision, but intimated that at a convenient opportunity she should shut her doors against them, and give orders that they were not to be let into the house. They were then unable to go out together even in the garden, as one was always obliged to stay in to open the door to the other. So they took exercise by turns, and went to church by turns, and visited the Cottage by turns. Meanwhile they consulted a lawyer, and begged him to consult with the family lawyer to see if Mrs. Selfe could not be persuaded to act reasonably.

Mrs. Selfe, seeing how determined her daughters were, took occasion to say to Claudia, who she knew was the most timid, that she need not fancy that by one of them staying in the house they could not be turned out, for if necessary she would use force and send for a policeman. Poor gentle Claudia, who had no knowledge of law, pictured herself being forcibly turned out by a policeman, and was in terror till her sister came home. After this, Manly Frowde lent them a big hand-bell, which was to be rung out of window in case of emergency, and he would go to the rescue. No emergency arose, though there was a false alarm. Early one morning Mrs. Frowde heard a bell. Her husband had just finished his bath.

"Rush, Manly, rush," she said; "get some clothes on, and go as quick as possible; there's no knowing what distress those poor girls are in."

Mr. Frowde put on a few things and went to the top of the lane, where he could see the windows of the girls' rooms; but there were only a couple of maid-servants making the beds, and looking astonished to see Mr. Frowde in such an odd costume, earnestly staring up at the house. It was discovered that the bell belonged to a gang of travelling workmen who were breakfasting at the Pleiades.

Mrs. Selfe evidently found her daughters too much for her at this period. Their merry voices were a constant annoyance to her. As she had entirely given up talking herself, except in ordering servants, it was a little annoying to hear her daughters talking and laughing with one another. So she invited to her house a lady whom she had described to Mrs. Frowde in their days of intimacy as a " very dear old friend."   This dear old friend was a Mrs. Naylor, a little fat old woman of about sixty.   She was what is called a well-informed woman—painfully well-informed—and was supposed to be very learned in chemistry.   Indeed, she had written a book on chemistry, but has not yet found an appreciative publisher.   Mr. Naylor was heard of, but never seen.   He was in fact a male Mrs. Harris.   His wife's allusions to him were perhaps not quite so frequent as were Sairey Gamp's to Mrs. Harris, but he was dragged in at convenient periods, as, for instance, when Mrs. Naylor was lecturing Claudia on the importance of obedience to her mother, even if her demands were unreasonable.   She said that she had always done what Mr. Naylor bid her, although it might not have been pleasant to

her. Considering the light in which she regarded her husband, perhaps it was hardly a
compliment to her friend Mrs. Selfe to com-
pare the two cases, for she evidently looked
upon Mr. Naylor as a poor ignorant fellow,
who was not fit for a companion to such a
well-informed person as herself. No doubt
Naylor was a jolly fellow, who, so far
from asking obedience from his wife, was
only too glad to be left alone. Probably
he enjoyed his glass of port when he was
beyond his wife's control. Mrs. Naylor
sometimes alludes to a "babe" she once
had (baby is too common-place a word for
her), but this babe, fortunately for itself,
did not live, or, to use Mrs. Naylor's own
words, "It passed away from life when
about ten months old." No other babe
seems to have been born; and really, when
we consider Mrs. Naylor's extraordinary
fund of information, it is astonishing she

could do anything so ordinary as produce a babe.   Mr. Naylor's occupation is never disclosed, but from an anecdote of Mrs. Naylor's, he seems to be something in the *travelling* line.   For she relates that once having appointed to meet her husband at an inn in a country town, where he would stay in the midst of his travels, she arrived at the inn before her husband, and asked to be shown into his room.   The people of the inn did not believe she was his wife, and refused to admit her, so she had to wait outside till he came.   Now whether Mrs. Naylor relates this to show that people at inns are not always courteous, or whether she thought she was so good-looking that she might be mistaken for a mistress, it is impossible to say.   It would require a great stretch of imagination to suppose that she had ever been anything but ugly.   It is curious that a woman of Mrs. Selfe's understanding chose such extraordinary friends. But the reason is evident: Mrs. Naylor is a toady, and Mrs. Selfe likes a toady. Mrs. Naylor will agree with Mrs. Selfe in everything. She did not even speak to Diana and Claudia in their mother's presence, because she knew it would please Mrs. Selfe; but when she found them alone she would enter into conversation, and if Mrs. Selfe entered the room she would suddenly stop and look guilty. And when at dinner she was asked to have a glass of wine, she would cry out, "Oh, plenty!" before her glass was half filled, because she knew that Mrs. Selfe was a rigid water-drinker. And now that Mrs. Selfe had a companion with her, the girls could not always get the best of it in the matter of talking. For if their voices were heard above Mrs. Naylor's they were begged to be silent, and allow others to talk. They ought to have considered it a privilege to listen to the conversation of their mother and Mrs. Naylor. And that our readers may not miss that privilege, we will here give a specimen of it.

Mrs. Naylor: " Have you ever remarked the beautiful harmony of form and colour in a blade of grass? I assure you that, without going deeply into the study of botany, you would find a knowledge of the various idiosyncrasies of our most ordinary plants a very interesting pursuit. For example," here she places the first and second fingers of each hand together to emphasize the words, " take the common groundsel—to the eye of the casual observer it is a mere weed; but viewed under the magnifying powers of the microscope, its beauty of formation is really almost startling. How much this proves the wise supervision of a beneficent Providence even in the minutest of His creations!" At this point the girls gave a sigh of relief, as if the prolixity of the sentence and the length of the words had taken away their breath. But they are the politest of ladies, as everyone knows who has made their acquaintance, so they listened for their mother's reply.

" A——h !" said Mrs. Selfe, with a drawn breath something between a sigh and a groan, like a converted Methodist, " it does indeed ! And how the progress of civilisation enables us more and more to discover this !"

Mrs. Naylor, profoundedly impressed with this truth, replies : " Assuredly so. This is indeed the age of discovery. What marvellous strides have been taken lately in the science of chemistry. Have you ever given your attention to the fusion of metals, and the influence of aluminum or lime-light on the ordinary oyster-shell ? It is, I assure you, a most interesting experiment, and the effect is really dazzling. A dear friend of mine, now passed from this life, a man of fine culture and poetic temperament, who gave much attention to this science, describing to me his feelings on first witnessing this experiment, assured me that he was positively affected by the dazzling nature of the light—in his own words, it was like a glimpse of Heaven."

The two girls, finding their politeness stretched to the utmost in listening to Mrs. Naylor, began to wish she had also " passed away from this life," like her dear friend. They endeavoured to turn the subject, and that they might still keep the conversation up to the intellects of the two learned ladies, they thought they would be safe in mentioning authors. But, unluckily, having mentioned Manly Frowde, they brought from Mrs. Naylor the remark that he was

too "latitudinarian," and that "latitudi-
narianism is not genius." Eight syllables
was too much for them, so they gave up altogether and left their mother and Mrs.
Naylor to converse alone.

The siege lasted about three months, and
then Mrs. Selfe, being anxious to get rid of
her daughters, and finding that they had
friends who would not allow them to be
ill-treated, gave way to the proposal of the
family solicitor that a suitable provision
should be made for them, and that they
should make their home where they pleased.
Most mothers will say that such a woman as
Mrs. Selfe does not exist, or that her daughters must be very bad indeed, and deserved
such treatment. All who know Diana and
Claudia are charmed with them. They
are as intellectual as they are beautiful, and
their severe life has made them full of
tenderness and kindness. They are de-

lighted with their liberty, and have taken a little farmhouse in a midland county, where they live together very happily. They have visited Mr. Frowde several times, though it was difficult to persuade Claudia to come at first, as she suffered for months after leaving her mother with a nervous affection. We must not omit to mention that when they took leave of their mother they went to shake hands with her, and said they would come to her at any time she wished.

"Oh, you will ! will you ?" she said, and these were her last words to them. No kiss or kind wish. They never remember being kissed by her in their lives.

CHAPTER X.

BRIGHTON ROMANCE.

Some hearts are keen as diamond,
Some softer than the rose :
Ah ! if they meet together,
And part in stormy weather,
How fast the life-blood flows !

THE amber-tressed, witch-eyed lady whom we have called Flora was known at the Grand Hotel as Mrs. Trevor. When she parted abruptly from Arundel Lifton, she by no means intended to desert the ball. But his cynical cruelty cowed her for the moment; and she ran up stairs to her own room, a sumptuous suite on the chief corridor—for Mrs. Trevor chose to live like a princess. Her maid, Estelle, had of course been watching the dance from without, and followed her mistress promptly. Mrs. Trevor was a creature of caprice, and it was nothing unusual for her to suddenly leave any place of entertainment. Estelle, a black-haired, black-eyed little French girl, sprightly though ugly, knew all her moods, and was astonished at nothing she did.

Flora threw herself into an easy-chair by her dressing-room fire, and buried her flushed face in her pretty plump hands, from which she had torn the gloves as if they fettered her. This man's contemptuous coolness maddened her. She was powerless against it. She, poor pretty little thing, had loved him, so far as there was room in her small heart for love : she adored the splendid style of the man, his lofty self-possession, the lordly ease with which he made his way through the world. He knew no difficulty. As to her, he had touched her lightly, and she fell into his hand like a full-ripe peach. Then there came the bitter-sweet delight of an unholy passion; then a cool dismissal, with most liberal arrangements. His words were too true: he had bought her, body and soul, and then thrown her aside in his first mood of weariness. She would have murdered him if she could.

Presently she looked up, and caught a glimpse of her maid reflected in the mirror over the mantelpiece.

"You are here, Estelle?" she said; "I came up because I was tired. I shall go down again, presently."

"Oh, yes, let Madame descend. The

room is not so crowded; the hum-drum people go away. Let me arrange Madame's hair."

Deftly the girl replaced some wandering tresses, and put fresh flowers from a bouquet on the dressing-table, and cooled the heated face and hands with some dainty essence, and brought fresh gloves for those which lay in fragments on the ground. Then from a casket of gold-stoppered phials she took one, and poured into a small glass an oily green fluid, and offered it to Mrs. Trevor, who drank, and was refreshed.

"You are a good girl, Estelle," she said; "I will buy you something pretty when we drive out to-morrow."

"Thank you, Madame. But will you not come down? The gentlemen are all in despair because the most ravishing lady of all has left them."

Flora descended, looking radiant and feeling defiant. She had plenty of dances. She went in to supper with a youthful peer—so youthful that he firmly believed she was as young as himself, though she might almost have been his mother. He was over head and ears in love with her at once, and showed it by blushing till he looked like a very pink baby, and by getting her every incongruous thing possible to eat and drink. She was forced to laugh at last when she found a plate before her containing lobster salad and a Neapolitan ice. The young noble was not at all disconcerted.

"Hem—you see—when a fellow's very happy—don't you know?—he's rather off his head, you see. I put some beer into my own champagne, just now, 'pon honour, and it was all being so happy, don't you know?"

"If you have put any in mine I shall not forgive you," said Mrs. Trevor. "Just taste it, and tell me."

He obeyed.

"Oh, that is all right! And now it has passed from my lips to yours. I kissed the glass—I did indeed."

"I fear champagne and beer is rather an intoxicating liquid," said Flora. "Come, shall we have one more waltz?"

The boy was but too delighted. He went home in a glamour of ecstasy, fancying this beautiful creature loved him. She, who had only been amusing herself, went wearily to bed, being passively undressed by Estelle, who managed her mistress to perfection. Flora slept a dreamless, health-giving sleep, notwithstanding her naughtiness—notwithstanding that hysteric moment when Lifton's contempt had driven her wild. Only a small brain lived beneath those amber tresses: only dull nerves worked through the lovely contour of that plastic form. It is the creature of small brain and dull nerve who cannot help being wicked. However, Flora slept; and when she woke about twelve o'clock Estelle was by her bedside with chocolate, and dainty rashers, and toast miraculously crisp and thin. In a vase on the table stood a superb bouquet of hot-house flowers.

"Whence are those?" said Flora, sitting up in bed with a white shawl over her shoulders.

"I know not, Madame. They came by magic, I think."

As Estelle had received a sovereign to place them there quietly, her truthfulness may be estimated.

"Bring me the bouquet," said Mrs. Trevor. She looked at it carefully, and saw within its fragrant heart a something white. An emerald ring was wrapped in a piece of paper, whereon was written, in a somewhat boyish hand—

" Flowers—for the goddess Flora."

" Can you guess who sent this, Estelle ?" she said, trying the ring on her finger at once.

" Madame, no.   How should I ?   Every-one adores you."

Flora lay there dreaming, with an amused smile.   She was an indolent creature, and liked to lie late in her delicate surroundings, making day-dreams of delight.   She had been a constant reader of the flimsiest French novels : she had intoxicated her little brain with the absinthe-prompted sen-suous love-lyrics of Alfred de Musset and Theophile Gautier.   She dreamt of herself as an odalisque, a bayadère—a Venetian lady in her midnight gondola, bound on some mysterious mission of love ; a wild Indian nymph, with dusky limbs, swinging in her hammock from a great tree above a giant river, and waiting for her lover.   Such fancies, caught from the subtle song-music, mere foam-froth of the brain, wherein the French delight, were her morning enchantment. She would lie with closed eyes, fancying herself Murger's Musette, or De Musset's Marquesa d'Amaëguai, or Gustave Nadaud's fairy Ursula.

Estelle, a restless French girl, used to wonder how her mistress, wildly eager in pursuit of pleasure, could enjoy these intervals of perfect indolence. Estelle had not been fed on the erotic literature of her country : she could read but little, and just sign her name. She had been apprenticed early to a Paris milliner, had shown such skill and taste that her mistress was sorry to part with her to a great lady who wanted a clever attendant. She had, on the death of her patroness, been engaged by Mrs. Trevor, to whom she was a faithful and attached servant. Yes, Estelle really liked her mistress, who was prodigal and kindly, and made the girl her companion. Estelle waited on Flora with absolute devotion, foreseeing all her fancies, and hastening to gratify them.

The indolent creature stirred by-and-by, threw off her reverie, stretched her plump arms, and thought she would face the sunshine. So Estelle dressed her, almost as a child is dressed, for she hated trouble, and her maid knew just the style that suited her, according to the weather and her complexion.

"Estelle," she said, trifling with a luxurious breakfast, "I want to drive before the sun is gone. I hate chill," she added, with a shudder. "You must come with me: look your best. I think I told them two o'clock; it is past that, surely."

"I will inquire, Madame," she said, and in a moment returned with, "The carriage

waits." And very soon they were out behind a pair of respectable horses (not exactly matching the superb private teams that
crowd the King's Road), driving up and
down the most wonderful sea esplanade in
the world. Mrs. Trevor was buried in
white fur, for all the world like a strange
snowbird with an amber crest; while Estelle, having the art of dress, contrived on
such occasions to make herself look much
more like a lady-companion than a lady's
maid.

Presently they passed a fine four-in-hand
—three chestnuts, and a bright bay as off-
wheeler. Flora, who, like Pope's politician,
"saw through all things with her half-closed
eyes," saw who was driving. It was Arundel Lifton. He did not even see her, nor
did Lord Arun, who was on the box with
him. That off-wheeler had never been in
a team before, and required Lifton's skill

and strength to manage. There were a good many of Lifton's friends, male and female, who would have rejoiced to hear that bright bay had broken his neck.

This turn-out belongs to Lord Arun, an enthusiastic young peer, whom his cousin Arundel is driving fast to Avernus. Arun is twenty-two, and has about twenty thousand a year, and does not know how to spend it, so it slips through his fingers like quicksilver. Lifton's great mining royalties are rumoured to bring him in three or four times that amount; but, though he spends money like a prince, he calculates to the last sovereign. He can tell at any moment, from a little memorandum book in his breast-pocket, what he is worth within a hundred or two; and it must be a complex question, for he has been a great investor, and has probably never spent half his income. He is a born calculator, with a Babbage's machine instead of a soul. Will he miscalculate for just once?

Young Lord Arun, who likes to outdo everybody in everything, has set up a famous four-in-hand, but does not drive it with perfect ease of mind. On the box beside his cousin he is quite easy, for he believes Lifton infallible. And Lifton can do most things. But the groom had remonstrated against putting in that bay mare, a new purchase, to drive along the King's Road. Lifton said calmly,

"Do as you are told, man. Give her room if she wants to kick. Put 'Short Tommy' inside."

Reader, can you place yourself in the position of a bay mare that, for the first time in her life, though heretofore she has known harness, finds herself with three others before a vaster machine than she has ever drawn, or helped to draw, trotting along that thoroughfare of multitudes. Never has she seen such sights; never has thong touched her on the flank with such decisive sharpness; never has silver bugle sounded behind her. If that mare's nerves are upset, who can blame her?

Upset they certainly were. As they returned eastward, just by the West Pier, her skittishness grew worse and worse.

"You'll never get her home," said Arun.

"Pooh!"

He had time to say no more, when a stupid flyman drew round from where he had been setting some one down right across the near leader. The fellow was not blind, only stupid with long years of adulterated beer. His wretched horse went down, and both shafts were broken. Lifton's off leader was an old hand, and tried to obey the rein; but the mare was frightened into madness, and kicked fiercely, and in pulling the coach across the road it took off the wheel of poor Flora's carriage, as she was returning from her drive. There was a regular spill. Lord Arun, seeing who it was, heedless of his own affairs, scrambled down to help the ladies. Lifton took it all in at a glance, and at once meditated mischief. But he was looking to the horses. The mare lay on her side, moving convulsively. The three chestnuts were still, though shuddering with excitement.

"Her back's broken, I fear, Tyrrel," he said to the head groom. "She would have jumped right over that carriage if I hadn't struck her on the ears."

"You are quite right, sir. And my lord gave three hundred for her."

Lifton laughed. He knew the value of money well enough, but it always amused him to hear people lament the loss of it. He called to a sergeant of police who stood near.

"Sergeant," he said, "I must shoot this mare. Keep the people quiet."

There came a pistol shot, and the poor creature's career was ended.

"I never saw such a gentleman," said Tyrrel to one of his mates. "In course it was the right thing to do, for the poor mare was in misery and couldn't live; but I shouldn't have had pluck enough to do it."

Leaving whomsoever it might concern to clear away the wreck, Arundel Lifton walked to his hotel, and sat down to muse. The idea of Arun's being taken in Flora's net delighted him. He wished neither of them any harm, but he had a heartless pleasure in seeing other people go wrong. His contempt for mankind was so great that you might imagine his race had been crossed by a fiend. He laughed heartily over the thought of Arun and Flora making fools of

one another. Both born to be fools, their
meeting was a caustic comedy from the
point of view of Mephistopheles.

"I'll leave them alone," he thought.
"She'll say nothing to him about me, for
fear of what might come out. She'll pre·
tend not to know me, I expect. Oh, what
a game she'll play with that poor boy, unless I interfere! He'll come and ask my
advice: the man who asks for advice writes
himself down an ass at once. He'll describe
her as a pure simple creature—so sweet, so
confiding, so intellectual! I can see exactly
what Flora would seem to that boy. But,
by Jove! the time goes on. I must write
some letters."

He sat down and wrote about a dozen
brief letters of business to various agents, in
some of them enclosing cheques in others
requiring remittances. Never a day passed
but Arundel Lifton was in communication

with the people he employed. Ringing for a waiter, he said,

"Send those letters to be registered, and bring me the receipts. I shall dine here alone to-night, at eight—fish and cutlets, and a bottle of Lafitte. If anyone inquires for me, I am not in the hotel, remember."

Then he went into a maze of complex calculations, which seemed to interest him strangely. He wrote a minute hand, and the figures ran beneath his pen with the swiftness of Atalanta. Had not the deep misfortune happened to him to be prodigiously rich, he would probably have been senior wrangler.

Meanwhile, Lord Arun and Mrs. Trevor —but really this demands a new chapter.

CHAPTER XI.

A FLUENT WOOER.

Little it matters how love's tale is told,
If comes therewith a radiant shower of gold.

FLORA was not hurt a bit, nor indeed was she frightened; but the incident was too striking a one for her to miss an opportunity. She fainted—that is to say, she sank languidly into Estelle's arms, with eyelids drooping, and had to be carefully carried upstairs into the hotel. A whole bevy of Brighton cavaliers attended her: foremost among them was young Lord Arun, who had fallen madly in love with her the night before, and had sent her a *gage d'amour* in the morning, and who now felt disposed to tear his hair because *his* four-in-hand had done this harm. There was a real sensation throughout the Grand Hotel, and all over Brighton, so soon as the news was known. Flora had been the belle of the balls—the despair of the men, and the envy of the women; and, by the time the dwellers in mansions at Kemp Town and Hove heard the story, of course it was stated that her injuries were so serious she could not live. But when Estelle had brought her to her room, and administered a glass of that mysterious cordial, she opened her eyes and sank back in her chair, and said,

"Oh, dear me, how dreadful it was!"

As a fact, Estelle was more frightened than her mistress; and she was also a little hurt, for the edge of a wheel had bruised her shoulder; but the brave girl said nothing, and tended her mistress faithfully.

Presently came a knock at the door, and a card was brought—Lord Arun's, of course. On it was pencilled, "May I see you? I am *so* anxious." Flora smiled, but did not blush or tremble: this boy's fancy amused her, but she had known a fiercer if less noble love. She said :

" He may come, Estelle. Do I look very bad ?"

"Madame looks charming," was the reply; and Lord Arun was admitted, and Estelle was glad to go to her room and bathe her hurt shoulder with warm water.

When Arun entered, Flora looked up at him with a lovely languor. She was no longer the gay bright rose of the dance : it was

"As if a flower should close and be a bud again."

There was dew in her eyes, a tremor on her lips, and a pained tone in her voice. This little born actress knew that for the moment she was the heroine of Brighton, and enjoyed the situation. She had been calmly studying how one of her French models would have acted at such a time.

"'Pon my life, Mrs. Trevor, don't you know?" said Lord Arun, "I'm mad my horses should have done such a thing. Are you dreadfully hurt? You always look lovely, you see, but it's so deceitful."

"I am only a little shaken, my lord—mentally rather than physically. The shock was sudden; but I am quite well, I assure you."

"By Jove! you know, it was awful. And I was so happy last night—never so happy, I declare—and now, 'pon honour, I'm the unhappiest man in Brighton, except the man that takes people's names down as they go into a ball."

Flora laughed at the comparison. Lord

Arun had evidently pitied the gentleman told off for that duty, unaware that nothing would induce him to emulate those whom he had to note down.

"There is no need for you to be unhappy," she said, softly smiling like Lalage; "I am well, though tired. And I have some one to thank for this beautiful emerald ring, which I found in the heart of a bouquet of flowers. I wonder how these came into my room."

"When a fellow's happy, you know, and he knows why, he wants to make the person he knows why—no, I don't mean' that —I mean he wants to make somebody know it. Now, don't you see? I was happy, Mrs. Trevor, and I knew why: so I went to Bright's—he's got some good things —do you like the emerald, though? It looks jolly, on *your* finger."

She turned it round.

"I wish it were a magic ring," she said. "A ring that would make you invisible; then you could go and find out everybody's secrets. A ring that would make everybody tell you truth: Oh, I *should* like that! A ring that would make people love you——"

"That," interrupted Lord Arun, "don't you see? Mrs. Trevor, is just what you don't want. I believe you've got such a ring."

"Lord Arun," she said, "you are both witty and polite. You are generous too; and I will keep your lovely emerald—as green as the shallow sea. But please don't give me anything more: people are so censorious. I'm obliged to be terribly careful, they *will* talk, and I have no father or brothers to protect me."

"Who'd dare to say a word, I want to know, against you? Might I, with your

permission, wring his confounded neck?
By Jove, you see, the world's full of scamps,
male and female, and you never know, you
know, who anybody is; but the scamp that
would say a word against you, you see, must
be about as bad a fellow as the fat man that
called himself Tichborne. I don't like fat
men, you know: do you?"

"I have not considered that subject," said
Flora, with a light laugh; "but I think not.
Fat men don't walk well or ride well.
They haven't breath enough to talk. Their
souls have more than they can do to keep
their bodies alive. Let me see, though! I
have heard there is one thing they can do:
they can swim."

"Porpoises!" ejaculated Lord Arun.
"But about those scamps—you see I'm a
very good hand with a horsewhip, 'pon
honour; and if there's anybody has said an
impertinent word about you, give me his

name and address, and by the lord he shall have it."

" Oh! Lord Arun, I did not mean that," she said, liking the young man's enthusiasm. "I mean that there are people who will talk about a solitary woman like myself, and that therefore you must not come and see me too often."

" I won't—no really, I won't—shall we say twice a-day? I could bring you some fruit in the morning and some flowers in the evening, don't you know?"

She clapped her hands merrily.

" How delightful you are!" she said. " Twice a day! Why if you were to come but once a week all Brighton would chatter about us, and either say we were no better than we should be, or else that we were en-gaged."

" I don't want to be any better than I should be, you know, and you couldn't if you tried. And if Brighton likes to say we're engaged, by Jove! don't you see? let the rascals tell truth for once."

CHAPTER XII.

FAUST AND MEPHISTOPHELES.

He is the devil, not of superstition, but of knowledge.

CARLYLE.

LORD ARUN called on his cousin between eleven and twelve on the day after the crash. Lifton, in dressing-gown and slippers, with his untasted breakfast on the table, was smoking cigarettes and looking intensely bored. Lifton was always bored unless he was doing some sort of mischief. Lord Arun's arrival woke him up, and he said, gaily,

"Ah, Val, how are you? You are a

youth of enterprise.   What do you think of the pretty widow? Have you come to breakfast?"

"By Jove!" said Arun, "*Did* I breakfast before I came out? Yes; I had some prawns and a pint of hock. No: that was yesterday. Positively, Arundel, I don't think I have breakfasted."

"The boy's in love," said Lifton, with a smile. "Come, eat some breakfast, and let me hear your adventures."

He lifted a cover, but everything was cold. So he rang, and said to the waiter,

"Bring something hot. I forgot about breakfast. Be quick."

"I don't think I'm hungry," said Arun.

"Nonsense. Lovers always are. There is no business in life that requires more nutriment. You may make a speech fasting, or fight a duel, or play roulette, or ride a steeple-chase; but never make love to a woman without a rumpsteak and a bottle of Burgundy first."

A second breakfast arrived. Arun found he was immensely hungry. Lifton's flagging appetite was revived by his cousin's arrival in an amorous state.

"I must drink her health in champagne this instant!" cried Arun, and rang the bell. "You never saw her equal. She's as innocent as—as Devonshire cream, and her lips, you know, are rosebuds and all that,—and as to her eyes, by Jove, sir! they gave me a pain just here," pointing to where he supposed his heart to be.

"Champagne is good for that malady," said Lifton. "And so you think her perfect? I knew you would."

"Why, you don't know her, you know, do you?"

"Know her? I know all women to be very much alike when they get hold of a young fellow like you, always looking at them through a rose-coloured glass. Come, we'll drink her health."

Arun tossed off the champagne, and re-filled his glass, Lifton watching him with a contemptuous smile. The part of Mephistopheles (hater of light) had been played full many a time, but never more consummately than by Arundel Lifton.

"She really *is* a widow?" he said, interrogatively, sipping his wine with deliberation.

" Oh, yes. Sad story, you know—didn't tell me, too heart-rending. Married by force to some old miser, who plagued her to death, by Jove! always jealous, you know—died suddenly of losing sixpence, and left all his money to charities—luckily forgot to sign his will."

Here Arun paused to take breath, and his cousin said :

"If she didn't tell you this rubbish, how the deuce do you know it?"

"Read it in her eyes, you know. She's transparent, like—well, like a tank in the Aquarium."

"Bad comparison," said Lifton; "you can't look into those tanks without seeing something fishy."

"You may chaff. You don't know Flora—she's as pure as—this wine, and as delicate as—as—a cigar ash."

"That simile deserves a cigarette, and these are real Russians. I am glad you came in with your story, Val; I was most awfully bored. Is the wind in the east?"

"Didn't notice, 'pon honour. East is your right hand, isn't it? Yes, then it is in the east—blows straight from the Bedford, you know."

"Ah, I daresay it's all right. You have woke me up, Val. You are the most interesting fellow I know, now that you're in love. It's wonderful how it improves a young man. I've never been able to fall in love myself: no heart, perhaps. I never met but one woman worth a man's regard, and I made her hate me."

A gloom fell for a moment on the countenance of this man, which never at any time looked cheerful. If Arundel Lifton could not love, he could hate; and a keen observer would have been horrified by the dark revenge that suddenly convulsed his features. Arun, at no time observant, was full of his passionate fancy for Flora. The champagne quickened his grotesque flow of eloquence.

"You must come and see her, by Jove, Arundel. What's that story—didn't we read it at Harrow?—of a judgment of beauty, you know, at Paris, about three goddesses? Never saw a goddess—gone out of fashion, haven't they? like big lizards and giants—but I'll back Flora against any of them."

Herewith he drank another bumper of champagne, and looked as triumphant as Apollo when he started in vain pursuit of Daphne, a story well told by Ovid and Matthew Prior.   Then he said:

"Good-bye.   Where do you dine?   I'm off to see Flora."

"What a charming young fool he is!" said Lifton to himself, turning round to the fire, and taking another cigarette.   Lifton possessed in perfection Talleyrand's two requisites to happiness—a hard heart and a strong stomach: but he had occasional fits of intolerable *ennui*.   When in this case, wine was no stimulant—tobacco, or even opium, no sedative: all he could do was to endure to the end.   It was not remorse, for he had none; nor dyspepsia, for his digestion would have suited a cassowary : it was more like the evil spirit which came upon King Saul, and filled him with a horror devoid of form or meaning—a vague, unfathomable depression, with no definite cause. Arundel Lifton looked moodily at the fire, smoking cigarettes without tasting them, drank several glasses of Chartreuse, yet felt no addition of warmth and vigour.

"I wish something would happen," he soliloquized. "Life is too easy, and I am getting bored."

There are men who are formed for a tempestuous life. It is just imaginable that in certain circumstances Arundel Lifton might have achieved a kind of gloomy greatness. Had he lived in time of revolution, his ambitious spirit might have caused him to grasp power with a resolute hand—to become a dictator or an emperor. He had no conscience, yet a clear judgment; no affection, but the wildest momentary passion ; no knowledge of the meaning of love, but the faculty of hottest hate. Only a few persons, however, did he deem worthy of hatred : for the mass of mankind he had a cool cynical scorn. Could Lord Arun, who, though flighty and thoughtless, was a really good-hearted fellow, have seen his cousin as he really was, he would have shrunk from him with horror. But Lifton had a curious fascination about him. Arun was one of many who admired him because they found him incomprehensible. When a man has a handsome figure, dresses to perfection, is brilliant in society, spends money lavishly, knows all the ways of the world, his acquaintances seldom inquire too curiously into his moral character. Lifton was known to have done one or two things that might possibly shock the clerical mind, but which in very high society were voted venial.

"Well," he thought, "I'll take a stroll, and see if this Brighton wind will blow away the blue devils. Val is playing his little comedy, I suppose: poor boy! the *dénouement* will be amusing—to me at any rate. How far shall I let him go? Would that trivial thing like to be Lady Arun? No; she shall not have that pleasure."

He strolled out on the Cliff. A real Brighton breeze was blowing, ruffling the sea, driving the white sails, making the ladies' faces ruddy, and giving to their dresses a bewitching disorder. It did not blow away Lifton's blue devils.

CHAPTER XIII.

CHRISTMAS AT COPSE HILL.

The mesmerizer snow.

BROWNING.

THEY all lay late in bed that morning. Certes, they had sat up into the short hours, chatting over many things, making verses for the huge folio lettered "Copse Hill Rhymes," which lay on one of the bookshelves; talking much nonsense and no scandal, and enjoying "the sweet o' the night." But they had to turn in at last: only the master of the house, when everybody else had sleep upon the eyelids, dreamless and calm, took pen in hand and worked away for an hour or two. "One hour after midnight is worth two before," he was wont to say: and on that principle he acted.

However, he was up at nine, for it was Sunday morning, on which day, for some mysterious reason, the post at Copse Hill goes out at half-past ten. By this wise arrangement the letter carrier is effectually prevented from going to morning service; so indeed is Mr. Frowde, who, having perhaps a dozen letters to write by 10.30, can hardly breakfast and reach the church by eleven. As the letters are simply carried to Two Bridges, about three miles away, and remain there till nine in the evening, this regulation savours not much of the wisdom of Solomon.

As we have said, they lay late, with a depth of sleep under them—the hypnotism of heaven. When at last they lazily went to their windows, and drew the curtains,

and looked out upon the lawn, behold ! it
was white with snow, and snow still fell in
thick heavy flakes, and all the evergreens
were loaded. There was a simultaneous
shiver, and everybody rang for warm baths
at once.

Who were these Sunday sleepers who
listened, let us hope regretfully, to the
church bell, muffled by the snow? The
hosts are Mr. Frowde and his wife; the
guests are Diana and Claudia Selfe, and
Frowde's cousin, Henry Branscombe—like
him in many things, except that he is not so
big, wears spectacles, and makes money in
a much easier and faster way than by writing books. It is almost twelve when these
lazy people come down to their matutinal
meal.

Diana and Claudia, dressed in perfect
taste, are warming their white fingers
before the book-room fire, quite ready for

the meal—half breakfast, half lunch—which is just now ready for them.

"What time did you go to bed, Manly?" said his cousin. "You don't look much the worse for late hours."

"I did not notice," he said; "I think it was about four. Come, Harry, wake up, and give the ladies some devilled turkey. I've a right to be lazy, for I've written a dozen letters this morning."

"Do you like snow, Diana?" said Mrs. Frowde.

"Not in the hunting season," she replied. "I like the sleepy feeling it gives one."

"Oh, so do I," said Claudia; "but isn't thaw hateful? I call it *mean* for that beautiful white snow, that makes Mr. Frowde's white pigeons look dirty, to melt away into a nasty filthy slush."

"By Jove, Claudia, you remind me that my pigeons have had no breakfast. These letters early in the morning are an offence against civilization."

Opening a French window, he threw handfuls of peas to the beautiful white birds, who came with alacrity and then fluttered away to drink upon a stone vase of water close at hand. White as they were, the snow made them anything but white; but a pair of black carriers and a splendid cock blackbird, that came close up to the window in search of food, were deeper than the hue of ebony.

"Look at that dear bird," said Claudia. "Shall I give him some crumbs, Mr. Frowde?"

"You're a black ouzel yourself, Claudia, so it's only right you should help your kin."

"I suppose that's a compliment," she said, tossing out some crumbs, which soon attracted not only the blackbird, but his mate also, and a hundred or so of sparrows, and two cock robins who immediately engaged in mortal combat, and a missel-thrush, and two or three greenfinches. Meanwhile an atom of a titmouse was clinging with his claws to a bit of meat, suspended by twine to an ash bough near, and pecking away with great satisfaction.

"I like birds," said Frowde. "What life they give to the world!"

"What is your favourite bird?" asked Diana. "Being a poet, the nightingale, I suppose."

"No," interposed Claudia; "the eagle, which soars with undazzled eyes towards the sun at noonday."

"You have been reading Milton's prose works, Claudia. I should think the favourite bird with you two girls is the lark."

"It certainly is," said Diana, gravely. "Our life at Millbrook may be thus defined:

we rise with the lark, we work and amuse ourselves all day, and are as merry as larks the whole time, and we very often get a lark in the evening."

"Rather different from your previous life," said Mrs. Frowde. "What a treat to be free! I wonder how, with such a childhood of tyranny, you are so full of energetic life. It would have made some people stupid for ever."

"There were two of us, you see," said Claudia; "and we kept up each other's spirits. I don't care to remember it. It is a luxury to be free at any rate, as you say; and we contrive to live a tolerably happy life."

"An ideal life, in my judgment," said Frowde; "you have no troubles, except when your pony or your maidservant gets too frisky. You have heaps of pleasant friends without any ostentation—people who like you for your own sakes.   You have a guide, philosopher, and friend in that dear old agricultural gentleman who rides straight across country.   When you find the winter evenings slow, you can write a sensation story, and illustrate it yourselves, or make double acrostics, or learn Latin for the sake of writing it on post-cards."

"That last is an excellent idea," said Claudia.   "Give us a *Gradus ad Parnassum* —is that right?—and we'll do it.   I believe that writing post-cards in an unknown tongue would make a great many village postmistresses go raving mad.   We'll take to Latin, Diana."

The snow fell fast.   They could hardly see the people returning from church.   Mr. Bonfellow had preached a short sermon—a wise custom of his: the two or three country squires were driving home to lunch; the commonalty were trudging through the heavy snow to their dinners of pork and bacon.

"Not many people in church this morning," said Frowde. "Hallo! Harry, what are you doing?"

"Making [myself useful," he said. He had stretched himself on the hearthrug, a favourite position with him, and was carefully placing chestnuts on the bars of the grate to roast. Suddenly one of them burst, and the fine flour came all over his face, making him look like a miller.

He jumped up as if he had been shot, and everybody laughed.

"That's a chestnut wasted," he said, "and no doubt the best of the lot—the fairest of the flock, in fact. If the particles could be carefully collected from my face with a spoon I think perhaps they might be utilized."

Saying which, he went sadly upstairs to regain his ordinary appearance.

"Now," said Claudia, "let's eat all the rest of the chestnuts while he's away."

The malicious suggestion was accepted at once. He looked, on his return, with horror at the empty bars.

"At one fell swoop!" he exclaimed, and went into the dining-room to get more nuts.

Snow is a pleasant and picturesque thing to watch; but when you are kept indoors by it on Sunday in the country it grows monotonous. The ladies must not use their fingers, and ladies hate sitting still without using their fingers. The men may smoke if they like; but neither Frowde or Branscombe liked.

Perhaps the greatest difficulty is to know how to amuse children on Sundays. Dolls and dolls'-houses, carts and horses, puzzles and games, and all the fascinations of the nursery, must be gathered up on Saturday night and put into a cupboard out of sight. Dolly may perhaps be most fondly loved and admired, be carefully undressed and put to bed, and as carefully dressed in the morning, six days out of the seven; but on the seventh day she is concealed in a dark cupboard, where her poor little mistress goes occasionally to take furtive looks to see if she is all right. Some parents manage to quiet their consciences by letting their children have a Noah's ark. It is Scriptural they say. Also a puzzle of the map of Palestine is allowed; no other part of the world would be considered orthodox. Our friends were discussing Sunday recreations when Harry Branscombe suggested that chess might be proper if the pieces had Scriptural names, but the ladies voted him irreverent.

The afternoon passed pleasantly enough. They turned over various books, read snatches of verse, criticized the critics, finally had some tea. Just as it was brought in, all the dogs in the place barked furiously, and they saw at the front gate a man on horseback. He rode deliberately towards the front door. Diana and Claudia watched him with all their eyes. He was a good man on a good horse—that they could see, being pretty keen judges of both horses and men.

"Who's this comes riding o'er the snow?" said Frowde to Diana. "I must go and see."

There was expectation among the ladies while the new-comer got rid of his riding-coat, while his horse was taken to a stable. He entered: everyone liked his looks: after a sharp ride he was glad of a cup of warm tea with some whisky therein. When he began to thaw he also began to explain himself.

"You haven't introduced me, Mr. Frowde," he said.

"By Jove, no more I have!" This was a constant failing of his, for which his wife was always scolding him. "Mr. Sebright," he went on; "met him at Venice—Mr. Sebright, Miss Selfe—&c., &c., &c."

"You're a nice fellow at an introduction," said Mrs. Frowde. "These two young ladies, Mr. Sebright, are the Misses Selfe, great friends of ours; and this is our cousin, Mr. Branscombe—and we are all delighted to see you, for your own sake, and because anybody would be welcome in such weather. Now let me order something to eat. You must be hungry after your ride."

"Thank you, just a biscuit or sandwich," said Sebright.

"And I am sure you will stay to dinner,

and remain the night with us," said Mrs. Frowde.

Sebright did not object.   When the order had been given, he turned to his hostess and said :

"My father and mother were called away the day before yesterday to my grandfather's brother, up near York, who is immensely old, and supposed to be dying.   My mother is his only niece, and I suppose he'll leave her a lot of money.   Well, they went.   I was left alone, with exactly nine people within three miles, and three of the nine as deaf as a post.   Well, I got through yesterday with a long ride, and dined alone without knowing what I ate, and went to bed early.   But before I went I thought of you, Mr. Frowde, and I remembered Mrs. Frowde's kind invitation ; so I gave my man orders for my horse to be ready to-day at twelve, for I was determined to come, whatever the weather might be.   I had quite forgotten it was Sunday.   I hope you don't think I am very wicked, Mrs. Frowde."

"Very shocking, indeed," said Mrs. Frowde in fun, "but you can receive absolution from our good parson, Mr. Bonfellow, for he is coming to lunch with us to-morrow."

"Have you yet made up your mind about taking orders?" said Manly Frowde.

"No, though my father still urges me," he replied.

"I suppose you spend Christmas with your family," said Mrs. Frowde.

"It seems very probable that my family will be represented entirely by myself, and that I shall dine in solitary state, with a turkey and plum-pudding all to myself."

"Oh, you cannot possibly do that," said Mrs. Frowde, "I must insist on your staying with us, if you do not mind our humble entertainment."

"Thanks, you are too kind," said Jack Sebright. "The fact is the mater always likes me to be at home at Christmas time, and we generally have a maiden aunt and a couple of cousins of the old-young lady style to stay with us ; but I heard from my father this morning that the old gentleman is much worse, and they are not at all sure of being home by Christmas day ; so they have put off my aunt and cousins. I can't say I'm sorry, for the three ladies think it necessary to lecture me on my undutiful conduct to my father in not taking orders."

"Then you will dine with us, Mr. Sebright, won't you?" said Mrs. Frowde.

" I fear that I shall be an intruder in a family gathering."

" We can hardly be called a family gathering," said Manly Frowde, " which is perhaps all the better, as there is no fear of lecturing or quarrelling."

"I must go home to-morrow afternoon," said Jack Sebright, "and wait for news on Christmas morning. If I find my father and mother are not coming home on that day, I will, with your permission, Mrs. Frowde, come over to dine with you."

At this moment Diana and Claudia went into the garden to find leaves and berries to wear in their hair at dinner. Harry Branscombe followed them.

Mr. Frowde's garden is separated from Winterslow by a lane. At the top of this lane is the entrance-gate to Winterslow; and nearly opposite is a small private gate into Mr. Frowde's garden, but so overhung with foliage that it is scarcely visible. It is seldom used, as there is no thoroughfare in the lane, and would only be of service if a friendly neighbour were living at Winterslow, as it makes a short cut between the houses. Claudia and Diana were near this gate, trying to get some ivy that had been protected from the snow, when Harry Branscombe shouted—

"Diana! Claudia! Look what lovely red berries there are in your mamma's hedge. Shall I go and steal some?"

"Oh! do," said Diana and Claudia both at once; and they rushed through the wicket-gate after Harry, and almost ran against their mother. Mrs. Selfe was coming home from afternoon church, and in walking up the lane had been keeping close to Mr. Frowde's palings, as there was a little path which had been kept free from the snow by the palings and trees above.

"Good gracious, Di!" said Claudia when they had retreated, "what will she say? She must have heard our conversation all the time. And oh, Mr. Branscombe! she will think us so wicked for allowing you to call us by our Christian names. Oh, I shan't dare to go out again while we are here."

"What nonsense!" said Diana; "it is no good to fret ourselves about her: it won't do any good. We have had misery enough, and now we must make the best of things and be happy. I shall not let her spoil my enjoyment."

There was a general good-fellowship amongst all the people who met at Mr. Frowde's house, and a preference for Christian names which would be considered very wrong by people who find it necessary to be ruled by fashion and ceremony. "Familiarity breeds contempt" applies only to people who cannot afford to be familiar.

What were Mrs. Selfe's feelings when she suddenly saw her daughters? It is impossible to say. That calm pale face shows

no sign of emotion. It is horrible to imagine
that a mother can hate her own children—
and only children. Some warm-hearted
mothers will say that it is impossible. They
will say that Mrs. Selfe must have loved her
children, and that they did not understand
her. It may be so; but the children certainly did not realize her love.

Mrs. Selfe dined in her usual solitary way
that evening.

"Missis looks duller than usual," said the
servant in waiting, to the cook. "I suppose it's because the young ladies are next
door."

"Poor dear young ladies!" said the cook.
"I wish it could all be made right, and they
could come home again, for I am sure they
mean no harm. But I daresay they are
happier away. It is a dull house for them,
with never any company, and no good
dinners to send up."

The next day Mrs. Selfe posted a letter to her house-agent, in which she told him that she had quite decided to let her house, and begged that Mr. Temple might be informed of her decision as soon as possible.

CHAPTER XIV.

THE VICAR.

THE OLDEST INHABITANT :
He has a natural Christianity
Born with him ; no deep theologian he,
With explanations of the original text,
To make the old women stare ; nor yet a fancy
For chirping boys with nightgowns o'er their jackets,
And lighted candles, stinking incense, mummery
The girls delight in.   No ; he's kind to the poor,
And doesn't ask them prying insolent questions.
THE TRAVELLER :
He's a good fellow.

Old Play.

THE next morning Frowde was busy, having work to get off by the post, and well aware that he should find little time between luncheon and dinner, with guests in the house. And, as Mrs. Frowde was engaged in those mysterious affairs of state which on Monday mornings seem to occupy married ladies who are their own housekeepers, the other four were left to entertain each other. The snow had ceased : the sky was full of light, and cloudless ; it was still freezing, and the pigeons, after vainly pecking at the thick ice in their drinking-vase, were scattered over the lawn, refreshing themselves with snow-crystals. The elastic air trembled with life.

"Can't we take a walk?" said Claudia. "There are two good hours to luncheon. I know the neighbourhood well, and can take you a pleasant tramp."

" You were lost in the woods once, you know, Claudia," said her sister.

" Well, we're not going into the woods to-day. Come, get ready, all of you. An hour out and an hour home will be eight miles."

"Good walking for ladies," said Sebright.

Yet they did it, meeting a keen east wind as they went, but religiously keeping to time and distance before turning. Sebright soon became a favourite. He was as full of fun as any boy. They ran races, and he showed himself as much swifter of foot than the ladies as they than Branscombe. He could not see a gate without vaulting it, nor an old woman without inquiring about her family, as if he had known her for ages, and giving her a shilling as a Christmas-box. They came to a long shallow pool, where the boys had made a capital slide, and were "flying the garter" with a crowd of little girls looking on. He tossed a pocketful of coppers on the ice, and soon the youngsters were tumbling over one another in a most amusing scramble. Then he went down the long slide himself in a masterly manner; whereupon Branscombe, not to be outdone, though he had never been on the ice in his life, tried to follow him, and sat down ignominiously, amid a scream of laughter from the children.

"Now, young ladies," cried Sebright, "come and slide! You've done it hundreds of times, I know."

Diana and Claudia *had* done it hundreds of times, and they could not resist the temptation now; and, faith, it was a pretty sight to see the two trim-ankled lasses flying along the ice, putting Branscombe, whose intractable feet would *not* keep together, to utter shame, and responding thoroughly to Sebright's school-boy exclamation,

"Keep the pot boiling!"

"What would mamma have said if she had passed?" said Claudia to her sister.

Oddly enough, the old lady had driven

past, and recognised her daughters; but they, breathlessly intent on keeping up the steam, were happily ignorant of it.

"Feel sore, Mr. Branscombe?" quoth Sebright, as they strode along, whereat the ladies laughed.

"Not a bit. I only came down five times. I believe with practice I should slide better than you do.'

Whereat the ladies laughed again.

The merry party came in warm and cheerful, hungry and thirsty, with reddened skins and tingling pulses. Fight King Winter while ye are young, and you will not dread him in age. The constitutions of men and women of a strong race like the English are capable of almost anything: but too often they are seriously injured in youth by mismanagement; and the present mania for rapid, and, in some cases, excessive education, seems likely to increase their injury. It was a saying of the Duke of Wellington's that a man might be educated beyond his mind. Physical education should be the first thing. Many of our ablest men have died before their time because their precocity was encouraged in boyhood to the detriment of their bodily health. Jack Sebright was an admirable specimen of the opposite system. The Rev. Marston Sebright saw that his boy was not brilliant; but he saw that he had sound sense, and that completeness of corporal form which is given to one man in a thousand—more likely one in a myriad. From his childhood young Sebright was encouraged in all manly exercises: he rode a wild little Exmoor pony at five; he swam by instinct when they put him in the sea; he boxed, fenced, boated, with a natural aptitude. Then his father began cautiously with a little Latin and Greek and mathematics, and Jack went at it as he would have gone at a ride across country. His memory, which really is a physical faculty, retained everything: his understanding, or .apprehensive power, was as clear in reference to what he had to learn as it was with regard to his physical pursuits; but his reasoning faculty moved slowly, and his imagination slowlier still.

"Never mind," said the Rector, talking over these things to his wife; "he'll mend by-and-by. He'll have to reason when he begins theology, and when he gets among the girls his imagination will be stimulated."

"Oh, Marston, what an odd idea!" said the lady.

"Which of the two, dear?"

She put down her knitting to reflect.

"Well, I meant about the girls," she said. "But the other seems quite as odd, for I never could see any reason in what they call theology."

The Rector laughed.

"There is a great deal, I assure you ; but it is much tangled by unreasoning people. Jack shall go at logic before he begins theology.   As for the imagination, why, it would have no work to do if the world had no women in it."

Jack Sebright had by this time gone through his logical course, and was perplexed by his course theological.   But his imagination still slept.   He thought Diana and Claudia, for instance, jolly girls, capital comrades, full of fun and wisdom ; he was particularly fond of ladies' society, and had a natural chivalry beneath his strong animal spirits.

The Vicar was in Frowde's book-room by the time the ladies were ready, and greeted his ex-parishioners with much friendship, and was introduced to Sebright.

"I have heard of your father often," he

said, "but we do not happen to have met."

"He stays very much at home," said Jack. "Being unable to do any work in the Church, he is rather disappointed: but he wants me to make up for it, and become a bishop, like my grandfather."

"And why not?" said Mr. Bonfellow.

But at this moment luncheon was announced—in a larger room than you would have suspected the cottage to possess, the design of the hostess.

"You must have found your walk cold," said the Vicar to Claudia.

"Not at all. We defied the east wind. We ran races. We enjoyed a slide. I am as warm as a baked apple!"

"Who was the best slider?" asked Mrs. Frowde.

"Mr. Branscombe," said Diana gravely; "and the best runner too. Wasn't he, Mr. Sebright?"

"Indeed he was."

"Harry, I'm proud of you," said Frowde.

.Harry only laughed. If he could not slide, he could do certain things of more value to himself and the world than sliding.

"The Wemyses have left, have they not, Mr. Bonfellow?" said Claudia. "Who lives there now?"

"A new parishioner of mine, of whom I know nothing except that he is a thorough gentleman, and has the house full of books."

" A bachelor?" asked Diana.

" Good-looking?" asked Claudia.

"Natural questions from ladies," said Frowde.

"I presume he is a bachelor or widower," said the Vicar, "since I saw no signs of a lady. I think he is more in your line than mine, Mr. Frowde, for he is full of pleasant but erudite talk, which I cannot always follow."

"If he is old enough to be a widower," remarked Diana, "I shall take no interest in him."

"Don't decide in a hurry, Miss Selfe," replied the Vicar. "He's a man in his prime, and a very fine-looking man too. My notion that he might be a widower was because it seemed unlikely that a man of his style should have reached his prime without marrying. But I am really no judge of character, I have seen so little of human life as yet. I gathered that he had been a great traveller and a great reader, and I really think, Mr. Frowde, you and he would suit each other."

"Has he many visitors?" asked Mrs. Frowde.

"Does he keep a carriage and pair? you should ask, child," said Frowde. "If he does, though he has got his money by fraud and expends it with meanness, all the carriage-and-pair people in the neighbourhood will call on him. I'll wager you a pair of gloves against a cigar that nobody but the Vicar and the grand old General has called on him."

"Not mamma?" said Claudia. "She likes anything new."

"Your mamma keeps a carriage and pair. So does the General—two or three, I believe; but he belongs to an age of chivalry, not to these times of meagre ostentation. Should I win my wager, Mr. Bonfellow?"

"I think you would," he replied.

"There's a saying of Savage Landor's," said Frowde, "that those who visit can neither do much nor anything well. I act on this principle, and very likely Mr. Forncett does the same."

"I have never read Landor," said the Vicar; "who was he?"

"The most distinguished man that was ever educated at Rugby."

"What an unfair reply!" said Mrs. Frowde; "he was a great poet, famous long before Byron, and was at Rugby long before Arnold was master."

"Did he keep a carriage and pair?" asked Diana.

"That seems a very important question about here," said Jack Sebright. "I *have* kept a carriage and pair—that is to say, a tandem cart—and should have been sent down in consequence, if my grandfather hadn't been a bishop. After that, who would not adhere to the Established Church?"

Dried fruit of winter had followed luncheon, with cigarettes for the gentlemen.

"You have not decided whether you will take orders?" said the Vicar cheerfully.

"I am sure you would preach well," interrupted Claudia, "and not be too long."

"I fear I should be a regular duffer, Miss Selfe. Well, Mr. Bonfellow, there are two strong reasons why I cannot make up my mind to be what my father and mother earnestly wish. I do not think I am fit to stand up in the pulpit to teach people older and wiser than myself. I am not thinking of the gentry. I could be satirical on their vices and follies, male and female: but when I looked down to the back benches of the church, and saw faces wrinkled with trouble, and limbs weakened by the toil of half-a-century, and eyes longing for a vision of heaven to console them for the long weary misery of earth, I should break down, Mr. Bonfellow, I know I should. What am I to teach such people? They are nearer God than I am. What could a mere boy like me say at the death-bed of an old man or woman who had known seventy years of hard work, and hard living, yet been true to the Christian faith all through? I dread the idea."

Yet the Rev. Marston Sebright thought his son had no imagination.

"Go on," said Frowde, seeing that he had grown quieter after a few puffs at his cigarette. "What is your other difficulty?"

"Creed," he replied. "What is truth? What am I to believe and teach, amid this conflict of creeds? Are certain genu- flexions and gesticulations necessary to salvation? Whom am I to follow, amid the innumerable teachers and squabblers of the time?"

"Christ," said the Vicar quietly. "Study the Gospels, and leave all other theology alone."

"Perfect advice," said Frowde. "De- pend upon it, Sebright, that your very scruples form a guide for you. The young fellow who takes holy orders without thought of these things proves his own unfitness. Give no more study to the Thirty-nine Articles ; take Mr. Bonfellow's counsel, and read the Gospels—*without* the commentators, who give you comparisons and discrepancies which are utterly valueless. Leave Paul alone for the present. If you want Christianity reconciled to the present time, read Coleridge's *Church and State.* I have a copy to lend you, but you don't want it yet."

"Meanwhile, will you lend it me?" said the Vicar. "I am sorry to say I have not read it."

"It is at your service. As to your other difficulty, my dear boy, I think Mr. Bonfellow will say that to see it is to conquer it. By no means dart satire at the front seats —at the wealthy squire whose cottages are pigstyes,—at the young hunting-man who would fain look younger, and who ogles the girls and wears a flower in the button-hole of the coat for which Poole is yet unpaid. The time may come for this. Preach first of all the gospel of great joy: speak to those who have endured toil and trouble of the exceeding great reward. I have no patience with satirical or damnatory or casuistical preachers, when the earth is full of the goodness of God as the waters cover the sea. There, that's my lecture; and the ladies are 'dratting' me, if you know what that means."

"It is rather a long story," said Mrs. Frowde; "but if you come over on Christmas Day, Mr. Sebright, there must be no theology."

"I should think not," said Branscombe. "Theology at Christmas! No. Roast beef, plum pudding, mince pies, devilled turkey,

punch, snapdragon, forfeits, mistletoe, and
Sir Roger de Coverley."

"Yes," said Diana; "and if you're a
good boy, Mr. Branscombe, when you wake
up with the grandfather of headaches on
Wednesday morning, I'll administer the best
of all possible cures."

As Jack Sebright rode homewards over
the snow—a long ride and a bitter one—he
pondered much on the conversation that
has been recorded.

CHAPTER XV.

FIDUS ACHATES.

Where will you find an honest serving man,
Staunch as Eumæus to the Ithacan ?
Foolish indeed the master who relies
On the new race of sluggards and of spies.

WHEN Mr. Forncett at length took possession of his new residence, he found everything exactly as he liked it. Ralph knew his idiosyncrasy, and had indeed come to like very much what his master liked— even to books. Not that he read such books as pleased Mr. Forncett: he loved travel-books, especially if full of adventure, impossible or otherwise. He liked Gulliver, and Crusoe, and even Münchausen; but perhaps his chief favourite was an English version of that father of historic romance, Herodotus. Indeed, he had read prose translations of Homer, and believed in all the wonders of the Odyssey. But modern books of travel also delighted him, and when Mr. Forncett bought new ones, they were always passed on to Ralph.

The Birches had been built by an architect (if that is the proper word) with rather queer ideas; the rooms were for the most part good, and all lofty, but some of them had no *raison d'être*. For example, on the left hand of the front door was a small room, which was dignified with the name of a breakfast-parlour. That room cost Ralph half-an-hour's reflection.

"Breakfast-parlour, eh?" he soliloquised. "The master wouldn't like that, I fancy. Why, he wouldn't have room to stretch his legs, much less to walk up and down now and then, talking to himself, or to me, or to Foxy." Foxy was an amiable but gallant bulldog who never took notice of anybody but his master and Ralph, and the expression of whose eyes were so menacing that no boy had ever had pluck enough to throw a stone at him. "No," continued Ralph, "that won't do; but the little hole will do well enough for my traps, and the window looks right up the path to the gate, so I can be ready for tramps."

It was one of the inconveniences of The Birches that there was no entrance for tradesmen; so that everybody had to pass the front door with their goods: this was among the minor annoyances which decided Mr. Wemys to leave. When elegantly-dressed ladies are being handed into a handsome carriage, a butcher's boy carrying a tray rather spoils the scene. It is odd how often country builders make this and similar mistakes in really good houses.

So Ralph took possession of what had been called the breakfast-room, and filled it with the things he liked to have always at hand. It was a heterogeneous assortment, not easily described; for in his wanderings with Mr. Forncett he had been accustomed to consider many implements indispensable which could scarcely be of much service in quiet Oakshire. Those workmanlike corkscrews have seen service in many lands, and will be useful in this still retreat, where wine and ale are not wholly forsworn; but those revolvers and derringers, with the brightest barrels in the world, are now on the retired list. A dagger of Toledo, " the ice-brook's temper," rests close to a many-bladed clasp-knife by Rodgers; a collection of tomahawks and boomerangs is in close proximity with cricket-bats and boxing-gloves. Ralph looks round on these and a hundred other things with great satisfaction : they all have their history, and he wishes he could write it down.

"What a book it would make!" he thinks. "I wish I could write like Captain Gulliver. It seems easy enough, when you read it : but only try. I wonder if that book-writer they say lives opposite, could put me up to the trick. Wouldn't it be rare fun on winter evenings?"

It was breakfast-time at The Birches, one fine frosty morning in January. Forncett stood with his back to a blazing fire, looking through a bookseller's catalogue, the only missive brought him by the post. Ralph had deposited a cover on the "footman" in front of the fire, and placed a coffee-pot in the neighbourhood of his master's seat at table. Between master and servant there

was an obvious likeness, such as may often
be seen in people who have been close
comrades for a long time. Ralph was half-
an-inch shorter than his master, and about
five or six years older; both had brown
hair and blue eyes—those pellucid eyes
which owe their strange brightness to temperate living and much exercise in the open
air. These two men had lived for many
years a life of easy activity, and were con-
sequently in first-class form. Either would
have started at once for a forty-mile walk,
and reached the end of it without weariness
and with a noble appetite. Both were
tough as steel, and liked muscular exertion
for its own sake. Mr. Forncett liked men-
tal exertion also, though he wisely re-
frained from giving the world the fruits of
it.

"I shall ride somewhere this morning,
Ralph," said Mr. Forncett, looking up from

his broiled game. "Grum hasn't had much exercise of late."

Now Grum was the cob, a most important member of the household. He was an Irish horse, of wonderful strength and cleverness; a rather dark chestnut, with a small white star on his forehead—a capital weight-carrier, with a fine stride and game to run up a stone wall.

Mr. Forncett rode Grum to the top of Copse Hill, and looked around him. How many a time, he thought, in his days of far travel, had he ascended some such hill, and seen beneath him the wildest scenery. An unexpected lake, a ruined city, with idols of a forgotten faith and inscriptions of an undecipherable language, a forest of enormous trees, a fissure in the earth of immeasurable depth, a camp of some wild people —such sights as these he had come upon suddenly. Now, riding to the summit of a hill, he saw the comfortable warmth and wealth of well-taxed, well-policed England around him. Here a great castle; there the grand stand of a race-course; at other points a military college, a lunatic asylum, the vast mansions of a duke, an ambassador, a newspaper proprietor;—on all hands towers and spires of village churches, centres of Christian love; woods alive with pheasants, long stretches of well-cultivated land, a railway to the south, alive with screaming trains. A kind of restraint seemed to surround him: he longed for a hundred leagues of prairie. He took the best substitute to be found—a canter on the common land which runs parallel with the high road for a mile or two eastward. It was the road to Medenhythe, which as yet he had not explored. When it opened out into a wide heath, with avenues and clumps of trees, which he saw would look beautiful in sum-

mer, he turned northward, and gave Grum
his head, and galloped till he came to a
quaint village close to the river—a village
dear to boating-men and brethren of the
angle, whose snug inns were ruled by friendly landladies, with wonderful recipes for
dressing eels, and for making the most
nutritious of pies. At one of these, whose
sign came from the Apocrypha, being indeed
Tobit's Dog, Mr. Forncett stayed to refresh
himself and Grum, being chiefly inclined
thereto by a desire to see what manner of
people he had chanced upon. By the aid
of one of the landlady's famous pies and
some good bitter ale, he made a hearty
lunch, and was surprised at its cheapness.
Then he rode home again, resolved that on
the coming of summer he would have a
boat on the river.

In this way, riding or walking, did Mr.
Forncett spend most of the fine days; and

luckily it was a fine keen season—weather
dear to men with strength enough to enjoy
it. If it rained, he settled down among his
books, and pursued various out-of-the-way
studies which were his fancy. He was, in
his way, a contented man : yet those studies
of his were very much in the line of Byron's
well-known requirement—something rough
to break the mind on. When Frank Forncett, years before, turned his face westward,
and made in time the circuit of the world,
he was haunted, whether in crowded city
or on solitary mountain, by one beautiful
sad face. It haunted him still. Not Care,
but ruined Love, sat behind the headlong
horseman, pursued the solitary walker,
dwelt in the library of the untiring student.
Time had mellowed the vision, investing it
with a soft and subdued melancholy; but
it held its own against all beauty of flesh,

all wonder of wit, all glory of apparel ; and Frank Forncett, for the sake of one woman who never could be his, treated all other women with a distant courtesy.

Just now, however, it becomes our duty to introduce him to a lady. Diana Selfe had strolled out one afternoon with Mr. Frowde to meet the postman, who brought that imperious necessity for a publicist, the *Times* newspaper. Mr. Forncett was at his gate, with similar intent. A slight altercation between the dogs led to the exchange of a few words, which gradually ripened into a brief conversation.

" I did not call on you, Mr. Forncett, according to country etiquette," said Frowde ; " first because I am nobody; next, because I have no time to call on anybody. At the same time, I am always glad when anybody in a neighbourly way will call on me, especially if they won't grumble when I am too busy to speak. I am a slave of the pen."

"A despotic master," said Forncett. "If I may look in now and then on you and Mrs. Frowde, I shall be glad. My only visitor just now is the Vicar, whom I like very much, and who comes from a good stock: but clergymen are almost as difficult to talk to as ladies—you are afraid of hurting their feelings."

"How ungallant, Mr. Forncett!" said Diana. "But if you can't talk to ladies there must be something intensely wrong about you—radically wrong."

At that moment the lord of the manor drove by a well-appointed four-in-hand, with his wife on the box, and powdered footmen statuesque behind.

"That's Sir Herbert West," said Frowde,

"a landlord of the right sort, and a most courteous neighbour."

"I can't see a four-in-hand without a shudder," said Diana; "there was such a crash with one right under our windows when I was in Brighton before Christmas. I hardly knew what happened: it seemed as if everybody would be killed, and the road was so crowded. Nobody was much hurt, I believe, but the driver shot one of the horses that was dreadfully injured. I never felt so faint."

"Whose drag was it?" said Frowde.

"Let me see. Lord Arun's, I think I heard. But he was not driving; it was a Mr. Lifton—Arundel Lifton. I think he is a member of Parliament."

"He is," said Frowde. "Good morning, Mr. Forncett. I must study the *Times*. I hope you will walk across the road when you are in the humour."

" Arundel Lifton," said Forncett to him-self, with a darkened face, as he walked down his path. "Why did not that fiend break his neck, and meet his proper punish-ment?"

Ralph, who opened the door when he saw his master coming, perceived that some bitter thought was troubling him. But it was a secret anguish, far beyond the ken of *fidus Achates.*

CHAPTER XVI.

THE TEMPLES.

In emerald meadows, slowly-winding streams,
Calm villages where peasants dwell at peace
    Around their ancient church,
    The quiet heart delights.
But rosy mountain-peaks that pierce the sky,
And cataracts shattered into diamond mist,
    And wild wind-tortured woods,
    Solace a passionate grief.

MR. TEMPLE was in the habit of making up his mind with promptitude; and, when he learnt from his agent that Mrs. Selfe had altered her determination, he gave instructions that the house should at once be secured. The departure of the old lady caused no particular blank at Copse Hill, where she had no intimacies. Her heart was with Garibaldi and Colenso and Voysey, and other notorieties of this irregular sort, to whom, sitting like a sagacious ghost at the writing-table in her wide bay window, she addressed long letters of advice and consolation. To the world around her she was something impalpable, intangible—a wraith rather than a woman—bloodless as Anacreon's tettix. She walked—especially in uncomfortable weather; she drove; she exchanged formal calls with a few of her duller neighbours; she read the *Daily News* and the *Inquirer*. When she vanished from the scene, the villagers thought no more of it than the melting of a snow-drift. She faded away for the present to Cheltenham, where a great Unitarian logician disproved the divinity of Christ every Sunday to large congregations. One such disproof might be deemed enough, but *Non credo* is as pertinacious as *Credo;* and even the believers in Nihilism can be enthusiasts.

Late in the evening of a February day the Temple family reached their house. Everything was in order, for Mr. Temple had employed first-rate tradespeople, and had sent forward two servants, Belgians, a man and his wife, to arrange the rooms as he liked them. The ladies were tired, and went to bed early. Mr. Temple sat up, alternately reading and thinking, till his neglected fire warned him to go also. He was wondering whether this last step could be made permanent. In his time he had seen many troubles, scarcely caused by himself—or, if in any degree so caused, entirely through his spirit of self-sacrifice. Mr. Temple was a stoic : he looked upon himself as a link in the infinite chain of humanity ; he thought of himself, not as William Temple, individual and independent, but as a husband, a father, a member of the State, a member of the Church. It was curious that he did not force this view on others: this was due to his belief that few men, and probably no women, are capable of accepting it. Of no man that ever lived could it be more truly said that "the heart knoweth its own bitterness." He would have scorned to mention the deepest imaginable trouble to his dearest friend. He might have taken for motto,

> "Si fractus illabatur orbis,
> Impavidum ferient ruinae."

This stoic had many friends, though strange events had urged him to a quiet life, and he saw them seldom. Once he had been a keen politician, and if he had pursued this career, would certainly have been a Minister. Even now, men of the highest political standing kept him acquainted with that inner current of affairs which does not appear in the journals, and asked his opinion on questions of a difficult character. He never wrote a line for the press; but his suggestions, passed by the Secretary of State through his secretary's secretary to an able editor, often appeared in the epic grandeur of leader type, and prepared honourable members for what they might expect from the Ministry in the course of that night's proceedings. No member of his family guessed at this. He possessed in perfection veracity and secrecy.

When he came down to breakfast next morning he found Kate ready for him, with bright eyes, and rosy cheeks, and rather dishevelled tresses.

"This is a charming place, papa," she said. "I have had Jack out for a scamper through the meadow and orchard, and very nearly got thrown, he is so fresh. I am sure there must be delightful rambles through those woods in the summer. I am afraid mamma does not like it so well: she says the scenery is too tame, and there are too many houses in the neighbour-hood."

At this moment entered the lady just named, and, with a smile of melancholy sweetness, took her place at the table. A woman more nobly beautiful than Leonora it would be hard to find. Superb masses of hair as dark as midnight were wound around a stately and statuesque head: her countenance was of the purest Greek type. The natural expression of her countenance was serious and serene: but there was in her dark eyes a dreamy wistfulness which spoke of suffering.

"Do you think you shall like this, Leonora?" said Mr. Temple. "It is very quiet."

"I could have wished a lonelier place.

And the grounds in front are so open to the road. Is it not a pity?"

"Yes," he replied. "The old lady, our predecessor here, was rather a leveller, I am told. She cut down the hedge in front, which was several feet higher. There were some fine old hawthorns in the meadow, but she disestablished them with great energy. However, I shall soon change the aspect of affairs. There is a first-class nursery about eight miles away: I shall ride over this morning and see what the man can do with laurels and hollies. If it does not freeze again just yet, we may shut ourselves in this spring. As to the meadow, I shall throw it into the lawn, and sprinkle it with ornamental shrubs; and in another year the place will look quite different."

"May I ride with you, papa?" asked Kate.

"Can you spare her, Leonora?" said Mr. Temple.

"Oh! yes. I want her to have plenty of exercise. She is just at the age when she ought to be physically active. Girls in their teens often take to brooding and dreaming if they live an indoor life."

"I don't mean to brood and dream, mamma. When I go to bed at night I dream of the morning, and when I say my prayers I pray for a fine day. I hope it's not wrong. The Church prays for fine weather."

"Go and get ready, child, and talk no more nonsense," said Mr. Temple.

Kate hurried off, and Mr. Temple said to Leonora,

"I do hope you will like this place, my darling. I shall not cultivate the neighbours, and they will not trouble us. If you do not like it, we will go elsewhere."

"No, William—no indeed. I want to stay here always. I am tired of wandering. If you like it, I am sure I shall."

"You will like it very much better when I have altered it a little. I will change it as if I had a magic wand. That pond shall be cleaned out, and lined with granite, and we'll have a fountain, and white water-lilies, and gold-fish, and Muscovy ducks. It will amuse you to superintend the alterations."

"I shall hate to go so near the road, William."

"Nonsense, dearest. There is nobody in this quiet corner for you to dread. Be brave, and forget these fancies."

"I will try, dear William."

"That's right. Now mind you eat a good lunch, and take a glass or two of wine. You need it, really."

Mr. Temple and his daughter rode away in the same direction as Mr. Forncett, as already described; but instead of riding off at a tangent across the heath, as he did, they held straight on through a turnpike gate kept by a clever bird-fancier, passed in due time through narrow-streeted Medenhythe, crossed the river, where lay a flotilla of steam-launches, and a few miles further on reached the gardens of which they were in search—gardens not surpassed in England for skilful and liberal management. Mr. Temple soon found all that he wanted, and arranged that the very next day the work should be commenced—always provided a hard frost did not set in.

"You must be famished, Kate," said her father, as he put her in the saddle. "Can you last till we get back to the river? There is a comfortable inn there, and we'll have some lunch."

"Oh, I'm all right, papa. I was so hungry with my ride that I ate half a fowl and such a lot of bacon at breakfast. Poor Lisette, who lives on chocolate, looked quite astonished."

Lisette was a French maid who attended on the ladies, and waited at table at breakfast.

The father and daughter cantered to the riverside inn, where they found eatable cutlets and tolerable wine. Places of very fashionable resort are a good deal spoilt by the miscellaneous character of their customers: nine out of ten are no judges of what is good, and accept without question anything that is expensive. The tenth, who is a judge, simply decides that he will not go there again. When Shenstone sang and Dr. Johnson perorated in praise of inns they had not been demoralized by railways: adulteration had not become a fine art. You could not get an elegant dinner at the old-fashioned English inn, but you could get a thoroughly nutritious one. Where is the modern hotel which will condescend to give you either the one or the other? Yet it is quite easy to combine both.

Shrubs and workmen reached Winterslow in good time next day; and, under Mr. Temple's active directions, there were soon signs of metamorphosis. The village woke up when it beheld the new family in possession, and a regular revolution in progress. The village inn and the village shop were both in a state of excitement. Miss Tattleton almost lost her character for omniscience, because she only knew that the name of the new-comers was Temple, and had heard from the boy (hired in the neighbourhood) that all the servants were foreigners, except Clope, the coachman, who never spoke except to swear at the aforesaid boy. Inquisitiveness grew furious, and when the village magnates gathered that evening in the bar of the inn to achieve happy stupidity by much beer and tobacco, the huge landlord came down upon the table with a blow of his fist, and expressed his opinion (not without an oath) that people who kept foreigneering servants were no better than they should be. No one contradicted Sir Oracle.

CHAPTER XVII.

PUBLIC OPINION.

I am Sir Oracle ;
And, when I ope my lips, let no dog bark.

"HALF-A-POUND o' 'bacca and a penny stamp, please."

"Why, what can you want all that 'bacca for, John?" said Miss Tattleton to her customer, who was the lad engaged to help the coachman at Winterslow; "surely you ain't going to begin smoking, like some of the bad boys of the village?"

"Be'unt for me: for Mr. Clope," said John, who had a very small vocabulary.

" And does Mr. Clope smoke ?"

" I never sees him," said John.

" And how do you like your new place, John ?"

John's answer to this was a grin of satisfaction.

" Well, do you like these?" said Miss Tattleton, giving him two big brown lumps of sweetstuff known as " brandy-balls," and which must have had a flavour of tobacco about them, as Miss Tattleton had just previously lifted her hand from the tobacco jar.

" Rather," said John; and he quickly stuffed one into his mouth.

To suck a brandy-ball being to John the height of happiness, he of course favourably regarded the giver of the sweetmeat, and answered her questions to the best of his ability, but felt a little puzzled to know why Miss Tattleton suddenly took so much interest in him, when she had known him ever since he was born and had not often spoken to him.

"How do you get on with the servants, John?"

"I don't understand they."

"Can't they talk English?" said Miss Tattleton.

"I dunno: they jabbers away so fast I can't tell a word they say; and Mr. Clope, he don't know neither," answered John, who thought he would ¦do his best in the way of a reply.

"And how do you like the master?"

"I loikes him."

"And the missus?"

"I ain't seen her."

"And the young lady?"

"She gave me a big bit of cake."

Notwithstanding John's anxiety to make himself agreeable in view of future brandy-balls, Miss Tattleton was no wiser at the end of the conversation.

But she thought something might be done with Clope if he could be persuaded to come to the shop; so she sent a message by John that she hoped the tobacco would suit Mr. Clope, and that she had sent the best she had.

John walked out of the shop, and was crossing the green to go up the lane to Winterslow, when he was accosted by Clope.

"Now, then, you young imp, how much longer are you going to be? If this is the way you do messages you ain't worth much. What's kept you so long?"

John had put the other ball into his mouth as he left the shop, and was now perplexed by four different sensations. There was the pleasure of having a brandy-ball to suck; but then how could he speak with such an angular sweetmeat in his mouth?

and what excuse could he make? and wouldn't his master be displeased with him?—for he looked upon Clope as his master.

"Please, sir," he said, the brandy-ball sticking out in his cheek, "she—she—she——"

"Oh, pray don't scold the poor boy!" said Miss Tattleton, in her sweetest manner. She had seen what was going on, and thought this a good opportunity of making Clope's acquaintance. "Pray don't scold him, Mr. Clope, it was my fault he was not quicker. I was telling him I hoped he was a good boy, and did what you told him, and what a lucky boy he is to have such a good place. You see, I have known him since he was born, and knew his mother when she was a little girl. I'm quite an old woman, you know."

"Don't you tell me that," said Clope,

quite taken by her manner, " you haven't seen the other side of forty yet."

" Ah ! haven't I ?" she replied; "and something more too. I've seen a good many come and go in that house," pointing to Winterslow, "but I hope we shan't lose you very soon. We want smart young fellows to brighten up the place a bit, and give us a little custom."

Now Miss Tattleton's pleasant manner, mixed up with a little flattery, so far overcame Clope that he made a few visits to her shop, the result of which was that Miss Tattleton learned that Mr. Temple was a quiet gentleman, who was very particular that everything should be well done; that Mrs. Temple seldom came out, and never went beyond the garden; that Clope thought she must be a second wife, as she looked too young to be Miss Temple's mother; and that Miss Temple was a very nice young lady, and always spoke kindly to the servants.

Clope, on his part, learned a good deal concerning certain of the inhabitants of the village, but the knowledge was not of much use to him, as he scarcely knew anyone by sight. He also found the people at the Pleiades very civil to him, and eager to make his acquaintance. One evening he went in for a glass of beer, when Biggins, in a heavy, good-natured manner, said—

"Well, coachman, glad to see you. Come in and sit down a bit, and let me treat you to a pint for a beginning; we always likes to give a welcome to strangers."

"Thank you," said Clope, and he sat down in the bar and looked round to see who were his companions.

"And how do you like these parts, coach-man?" said Biggins.

"It looks pretty fair. I shall know

better when I've tried," answered Clope.

"Well, here's your good health," said a little sharp man, who was also a coachman, and spoke in a rapid way, with a strong Irish accent. "I hope you'll find your place as good as I find mine. I've got a downright good master, who keeps a hunter for me to ride, and lets me do pretty much as I like. I found the missis rather a tough 'un at first, but I soon came over her; and if I don't turn them out as neat as any gentleman and lady in the county, my name's not Paddy O'Bryan."

"Yes, you're in good luck; you know which side your bread is buttered. But I wonder you don't frighten them, driving that brougham at such a pace," said Biggins. "Now, coachman," he said, "take another pint; it's the first night, and I never charge anything first nights. Perhaps you'll be able to do me a good turn some time or other.

I'm a carrier, you know, and bring everything right down from London up to your gate— not like those confounded railways, that leave you to send miles to a station. Come, take another glass."

"Thank you," said Clope, who thought Biggins a jolly good-natured fellow. "I'll give you a turn when I have the chance."

"What I says," said Biggins, "is, let us live and let live. Bless you, I'm willing to serve my neighbours and not make no enemies; but that there fellow over there" (and Biggins swore his usual oath) "must go a-interfering with everyone. Why, I believe if he knew I bought a bird or two from some poor fellow who had picked 'em up when they've been knocked over by the telegrapht wires, he'd have me took up for encouraging poaching. Poaching, indeed! what right has Sir Herbert West or any other man to prevent a poor man from picking up a bird that has been killed by the telegrapht? Or, for the matter of that, why shouldn't a poor man knock down a bird or a hare when he sees one in front of him? D——n the game laws, says I; we want old Garry over here to alter all that."

"I never saw such a crop of turmuts in all my life, only the rabbits got in among 'em," said an old man huddled up in the corner, and who was rather thick in his speech; but nobody took any notice of his remark.

"I don't think Garibaldi could do much with the game laws," said an intelligent-looking young man, who had ambitions that the village could not gratify, and came to the Pleiades for change of scene.

"The question of the game laws is a diffi-cult one," said a middle-aged man, who wore a wig of a colour too dark for his complexion, and who spoke in a dignified and dogmatic manner, as though in the habit of laying down the law. He had altogether the air of being superior to his company, and preferred to drink from a glass instead of a mug. "There is a great deal to be said on both sides."

"If you'd seen that field of turmuts before they rabbits got in," said the old man, taking advantage of a pause.

"Well, you see," said a big old farmer who had a touch of humour in him, disregarding the talker on turmuts, "if the game wasn't preserved there'd be none to knock down."

"Right you are there," said Biggins.

"I must say I like a rabbit—especially when it don't cost anything," said Paddy.

"And a hare's better still," said the intelligent young man.

"Rabbits are very well when they don't

eat up all your turmuts. If you'd seen they turmuts," said the old man.

"You'd better bring us a sample," said Biggins, at which there was a roar of laughter. But the old man shook his head with melancholy wisdom, saying once again—

"You never seen such turmuts, till they darned rabbits got at 'em."

Presently some of the company rose to go, Clope being amongst them. The burly Boniface was very friendly indeed, and seemed loth to let him go.

"All the best company comes here, coachman," he said. "We're a regular club of good fellows every night. Why, there's your butler, Paddy,—if he isn't a gentleman I don't know one; and there's Squire Ashley's footman, he looks in every morning regular."

Thus talking, Biggins showed Clope the

way to the door, giving him a friendly nudge at parting, and a pressing invitation to come again soon. But when he returned to his bar, and sat down with heavy emphasis, he grunted out an oath and said—

"I don't think that fellow's good for much, Paddy. A nice lot we're getting about here. Look at that servant of Forncett's, he don't condescend to enter a public, and yet his master can't afford to keep a carriage. The gentry haven't got any money now-a-days, or if they have, they're afraid to spend it. Now, if old Garry was to come over here, we should get our farms without paying any rent, and them lazy baronets and lords would have to work for their living."

A scientific student of enthusiasm might find much matter for thought in the influence which Garibaldi has had on people totally different from each other. Here,

with but one house between them, were
that refined and thoughtful lady, Mrs. Selfe,
and this heavy illiterate landlord, both
holding a strange irrational faith in the
Italian adventurer. The lady corresponded
with his admirers, grew the grapes of
Caprera, had on her wall his portrait, with
the ridiculous motto, immortalized by Mar-
tinus Scriblerus,

"None but himself can be his parallel."

She had dreams, doubtless, of a universal
republic and a Unitarian Church—of mon-
archy and superstition wholly abolished, of
a quiet, well-ordered, temperate, drab-
coloured community : and all through Garibaldi. But the stout landlord, who had
inscribed the hero's name in large letters
on his favourite furniture-van, dreamt of
quite other things. His millennium included
the abolition of rent, taxes, policemen, and

the game laws—a jolly time, when poaching should be legal, and public-houses always open. How the triumph of Garibaldi could produce two such very different results the lady and the landlord may settle between them.

"I don't think much of the new people we're getting about here," said Biggins, still somewhat irate with Clope, who had not responded to his cordiality with any effusion, being, in fact, one of those people who prudently doubt too gushing a civility. "They're a queer lot, all of them, Paddy, and as stingy as the devil. I don't believe there's a gentleman about here as buys as much good beef and mutton as I do."

"You want a lot," said the lithe Irishman, who was about a third of the massive landlord's weight. "There's no keeping up a fine figure like yours on bacon. I should say, now, you were heavier than Sir Roger."

This was adroit flattery, though it might not appear so to everyone. Strange to say, after Garibaldi, Biggins most revered the "unhappy nobleman" in Dartmoor: it was a proud recollection that he had once been mistaken for him; and Paddy's last remark resulted in his getting a final drop of brandy and water without the ceremony of payment.

CHAPTER XVIII.

FIRST LOVE.

The very first
        Lip that has slaked its thirst
At virgin spring
        As yet unruffled by the wild bird's wing,
The very first
        Bold mariner who burst
With shallop free
        Into a magic solitary sea.

IT was a breezy March day. The fast-budding trees were tossed by an awakening wind. Thrush on tree-summit found it hard to cling and sing, but conquered the difficulty, being strengthened by the ecstasy of vernal love. White violets were covering the banks, and in the meadows grew innumerable daffodils,

> "That come before the swallows dare, and take
> The winds of March with beauty."

On this joyous restless day, Jack Sebright, feeling as restless as the mad March wind, rode over to call on Frowde. As he came along the primrose-yellowed lanes, he sang and shouted. He was in exuberant spirits. He had a presentiment of some happy event. It was one of Frowde's idle mornings, as he knew; and he anticipated a pleasant gossip about things in general and his own uncertain career in particular. He liked to imagine for himself every kind of career that is open to an English gentleman; and there was no one of them which he did not feel disposed to pursue rather than that clerical career on which the Rev. Marston Sebright had set his heart for him.

When he reached Copse Hill he found

the Vicar at Frowde's cottage. He came with news that his parishioners, for their own sakes, were sorry to hear. A living a few miles away had been offered him, and he had decided to accept it. The parish was ancient, with a noble church and venerable traditions—the income better, the parsonage larger, which to a clergyman with a growing family is matter of moment. Everybody in Copse Hill was glad for Mr. Bonfellow's sake; and it was pleasant to know that he would still be a near neighbour.

"What a pity you had not made up your mind before now, Mr. Sebright, and taken holy orders! You might have succeeded me, perhaps—and it would have been a good beginning, as you like the place so well. Moreover, you might have persuaded Mr. Frowde to come to church oftener. I cannot get him to come, though I have often tried. He says the church is too hot in summer and too cold in winter. There is an old Act of Parliament, which I believe has never been repealed, which imposes a fine for non-attendance at church. Don't you think you deserve to be fined?" said Mr. Bonfellow, turning to Manly Frowde.

" I would pay the fine right willingly if I were a landed proprietor, or millionnaire, or railway director, or capitalist in any shape. It is the duty of such people to go to church regularly. But you see my brain is my capital, and I am compelled to work on Sundays as well as weekdays, and an hour in an ill-ventilated church would spoil at least one day's work for me. But your conscience may be clear on the matter, Mr. Bonfellow: you have done your duty in exhorting me. Perhaps your successor may be more successful."

" I am sure I hope he may," said Mr. Bonfellow, in a serious kindly way.

"Do you yet know your successor?" asked Manly Frowde.

"Yes, I believe a Mr. Voyd has had the offer. I am not very intimate with him, though he is a curate in the adjoining parish; but he is said to be an orthodox and energetic Churchman. He comes very highly recommended by the bishop of the diocese in which he had a previous cure."

"Is his name Vypar Voyd?" asked Sebright.

"Yes," replied the Vicar. "He is at present a curate of Mr. Urgent's at Battlefield, one of whose daughters he married."

"I knew him slightly at Oxford," said Sebright. "He was older than I, but we had some common friends. I should think he would make an admirable clergyman."

"So everyone says," remarked the Vicar, "and I am glad to have your independent testimony. I hope Mr. Voyd will make up for my shortcoming."

"Don't be unnecessarily humble," said Frowde. "If your successor surpasses you, he won't make us forget you. You were never meant for the Church, in my opinion, but you do the work better than some of the predestined parsons who were cradled in surplices."

"I don't quite know what I was intended for," said the Vicar, with a good-humoured laugh, "but I think I was put into the Church because I am the fool of the family."

"Nine men out of ten get into the wrong place," said Frowde. "The thing is to stick to your work, whether you like it or not. At the outset of life, if we have free choice, we have not the knowledge to choose aright. Here is Sebright; his father wants him to take orders, and I believe he will make a capital clergyman. A clergyman wants an unshakeable faith in God, and wide sympathy with humanity. My friend Jack has both, or I'm much mistaken."

The Vicar, who was carrying the news of his departure to his parishioners, soon took leave, and Frowde and Sebright started for a stroll.

"It is astonishing how I vacillate," said Sebright. "It is a great thing to be a good clergyman, of course, but there are so many things for which I fancy myself fitter: a soldier, for instance, or a sailor."

"You're too old for the navy, my friend, and neither service is worth anything unless there is war. You were not made to wear a red coat and gold epaulettes."

"Was I meant for a black coat and an M.B. waistcoat?"

"That remains to be seen. At any rate, in the Church you will see active service. I don't think you would do for a doctor or a barrister : your character is too simple for success in a subtle profession. You could not humbug a hypochondriacal patient, or plead with passionate earnestness for a client whom you knew to be guilty. Now simple honesty, which is a disadvantage in many professions and trades, is of real value to a clergyman. I don't say it will make you a bishop."

"Me a bishop!" interrupted Sebright, with a mighty laugh. "Jack Sebright in lawn sleeves and a silk apron! *Nolo epis-copari*, thank you, Frowde."

As they talked, they had been slowly ascending Copse Hill, where the path was narrow and steep. Just at this moment they encountered Kate Temple on her pony, picking her way downward. Her bright hair was blown loosely over her blue riding habit; her eyes were full of life and laughter; she was as gay and joyous as the coming spring. Frowde and Sebright both turned round when she had passed—possibly to enjoy the pretty bird's eye view of the village below.

"A pretty little girl, that," said Frowde, when she had reached the road. "She is the daughter of a Mr. Temple, who, you know, has just taken that ugly bay-windowed house where Mrs. Selfe lived. Don't you think her rather pretty, Jack?"

"She's not very little," said Jack, evading the question.

"Well, I mean she's a mere child—some seventeen or eighteen years old, I should think. She cannot be very old, for her mother, whom I often see in the garden from my bed-room window, does not look more than thirty. I should have supposed she was a step-mother, but that I see a decided likeness. She is a glorious-looking creature."

" Isn't she ?" said Jack, abstractedly.

"The mother I mean," said Manly Frowde.

"Ye—es," muttered Jack, in some confusion.

That day as Jack rode home through the Oakshire lanes he felt uneasy, and could not quite tell what was the matter. He slashed fretfully with his riding-whip at the young green shoots of hawthorn in the hedges, and muttered a good deal to himself. His brown mare Bessie once or twice looked round to see what was the matter, when her master made a more than usually vigorous dash at a hawthorn twig. At last she seemed to catch her master's spirit, and became restive too.

"Now, then, Bessie, old girl, steady, steady," he said. "Wonder what her name is?" he muttered. "Be steady, I tell you," he said aloud to Bessie.

Whether Bessie had caught her master's fit of restlessness, or whether she fancied he was not paying her so much attention as usual, and that she would devise some means to attract his notice, it is impossible to say. She had made several mild remonstrances at first by turning her head round to see what was the matter; and at last she became so troublesome that Jack determined to take the nonsense out of her. So he put her at the first practicable fence, and went home across country. He took the nonsense out of his mare, but he did not succeed with himself.

Mrs. Sebright, who was always cheerful, was very inquisitive that evening about Jack's friends at Copse Hill, and Jack was in no mood for answering questions.

"Don't you think, my dear," she said, "that as I am within driving distance, I ought to go and call on your friends, as you

have received such hospitality from them?
If we put the horses up at Copse Hill for a
rest and a feed, we could manage it very
well, though the journey there and back
would be rather long for them." Mrs.
Sebright was always over-careful with her
cattle.

"The horses wouldn't hurt," said Jack,
impatiently; "but you know I have told
you several times that Mr. Frowde does not
care for ceremony, and he never calls anywhere. I am sure he'd be delighted to see
you if you happened to be passing that
way."

" A little observance of ceremony is necessary sometimes," said Mrs. Sebright, rather
chidingly—meaning, no doubt, that Jack at
that moment was not very ceremonious in
his tone to her.

" Eh ? what ? ceremony ? marriage ceremony ?" said Mr. Sebright, opening his eyes,

after his after-dinner nap. He always tried to persuade himself that he did not go to sleep after dinner, but simply closed his eyes to rest them. He would generally catch up the end of a sentence as he woke, to show that he had been listening.

" Are you talking of the marriage ceremony, Jack ?" he said; " why, it's no good for you to think of a wife till you've found something to do."

" No, father," said Jack, laughing, though marriage seemed certainly the best form of ceremony to Jack at that moment; " no, I was saying that Mr. Frowde won't mind your not calling on him, as he doesn't stand on ceremony."

" Oh, ah !" said Mr. Sebright, " Frowde, ah ! clever man ! should like to meet him some day. Good scholar ! done a great deal for the Church in his time."

" Why, father, Mr. Bonfellow, the vicar

of Copse Hill, was saying he never could get him to go to church."

" Very likely, my boy, very likely : these men are often odd in their habits. But I should like to see him, for all that."

When Jack went to bed that night he could not sleep—a most unusual thing for him. He tossed about, and threw off some of the bed-clothes, declaring they had made his bed warmer than usual; then he walked up and down the room ; then he tried to read. He felt so feverish that he dipped his head in cold water : then he took a saline draught.

But there is one fever which cold water and saline draughts will not cure : and Jack was now realizing this—the Fever of Love.

CHAPTER XIX.

JEST OR EARNEST ?

False words in jest are spoken,
And hearts are thereby broken :
Ah me! it is a token
    That Love hath bitter times !
Ay, but pure Love's strong splendour,
Its utter soul-surrender,
Eyes true 'neath eyelids tender,
    Shall live in loyal rhymes.

VALENTINE LORD ARUN maintained his pursuit of Flora Trevor with gallant pertinacity. He did not know what to make of the dainty coquette, whose nature was as changeable as an April day. Arun had never learned to make up his mind about anything. His intellect was discontinuous, and moved by impulse: for this reason all attempts to give him an education up to the average had wholly failed. His tutors, though baffled, could never lose temper with him, his natural good-humour being inexhaustible. He was the first to laugh at his own incapacity. He could not spell. He could not add up a column of figures accurately. He never travelled much beyond the verb *Amo* in Latin. French he liked, and read Paul de Kock and Alfred de Musset: moreover, in English literature he read comedies of the Caroline school, Etherege and Farquhar and Wycherley; also he read *Don Juan*. And though his talk was disconnected, he wrote a pleasant letter—misspelt and almost illegible, yet with a vein of humorous gossip. Indeed, though his mere acquaintance would not have believed it, a few of his friends were aware that he had a knack at rhyme, and could hit off an epigram or any such trivial matter with happy effect. Arundel Lifton was in the habit of advising him to marry a clever woman, and get her to educate him. Val, who preferred pretty women to clever ones, showed no sign of taking this advice.

The game of caprice and coquetry was pleasantly enough played between Lord Arun and the fair Flora for a month or two at Brighton. Lifton was an apparently disinterested spectator. He chaffed his cousin mildly when they came together, and rallied him on taking so long a time to win a widow. Indeed, Flora was, in Lord Arun's own opinion, rather difficult. She would be all sweetness at night—all indifference in the morning. Sometimes he seemed to look through her blue eyes into her very heart; sometimes her reckless manner appeared to show that in moulding her fairy form the heart had been omitted. Did she know anything about it herself? It was doubtful.

On a windy March morning, with occasional bursts of rain from the east, Mrs. Trevor, in a waterproof wrapper, was standing at the seaward end of the West Pier. She looked out at the wild waste of shuddering sea, over which the lights and shadows chased each other in swift career. She was the only person on the pier. Very few indeed were on the unparalleled promenade of our English Baiae; for when rainy squalls from the east come down upon Brighton no umbrella will last an instant, and you are wet through almost before you know it is raining. Flora looked over the sea—a little sadly. Her gay and reckless temper was not long to be subdued: but if your brain is as light as a dove's feather, and the blood in your heart as effervescent as champagne, you must needs be serious now and then. Yes, Flora was serious. She thought to herself,

"We have been playing fast and loose, and now it is over. We have been flirting gaily under the eyes of that fiend, Arundel. He means me mischief, I know. He would like me to bring Valentine to the point, and accept him, and then crush me. I will not be crushed, strong and cruel as he is. No; I will tell Valentine to leave me."

"I must. If he knew all he would scorn me. It is hard, hard, hard! I think I love him as well as ever I could love any man. Shame that it was—to marry me when I was a baby to that cold austere man, who has spoilt my life! Oh! if I had known anyone like Valentine then! And yet he thought he did his duty by me.

Duty! I hate the word. However, I must do mine—and here comes Val."

She had heard Lord Arun's quickly approaching step. He came quite gaily through wind and rain, defiant of both in his blue pilot-coat with yacht-club buttons. He held out his hand to her gaily, and and said—

"Capital weather, Flora, eh? Fools stay indoors by the fire, and wait for the wind to stop. You're—by Jove, you know —just like a—what is it?—mermaid?—no, they're half fishes, ain't they?"

"A charming compliment, Val," she said, "I'm not a mermaid, sir. Well, have you and your black-looking cousin decided when you go to London?"

"Yes—have we?—oh, yes, we drive up to-morrow. Arundel hates railways—he's got so many shares. Yes—by Jove—to-morrow—unless——"

"Unless what?" she said, laughing.

"Oh, you know, Flora. Don't you see, when a fellow—you know the sort I mean —has a lot to say and it breaks into bits like thin ice when you're skating, you know —any other fellow, lady I mean—might help him out, by Jove."

"Out of the water when the ice breaks, you mean? Well, Val, you've broken the ice. I'll be frank with you: I am not good enough for you."

"Oh! I say—by Jove!" he interposed.

"True," she said, with a pretty little sigh. "I don't say I'm very wicked, but I'm not good enough to be Lady Arun."

"Confound it, now!"

"Confound it, by all means. I don't say I never shall be good enough. If I am, I'll tell you so frankly. Come, Val, don't be cut up. We've had a happy time: don't let us end it miserably. You go to London, and make speeches in the House of Lords."

"Hang the House of Lords! I should make a speech like—like a dying rushlight. 'Twon't do, Flora. I should say—'Well, my lords, look here, you know—it mayn't be the question before the House, but I'm in love, don't you see—and the lady won't have me, and won't say why—so I vote she's committed for contempt of court, and I'm committed along with her.'"

Flora laughed gaily.

"I shall read that speech in the *Galignani*, no doubt, and there will be an article in the *Débats* on it, to show that English wit is inferior to French."

"*Galignani?*" he said.

"Yes, I am going to Paris for a week too. Don't look pathetic: I won't forget you. We will be good friends, whatever happens: perhaps we may be better friends some day. But we must wait, Val. And remember how young you are : you may see somebody delightfully beautiful, of your own rank, that will make you forget poor little me."

"Never!" he said, squeezing her little rosy leaflet of a hand, and looking earnestly into those capricious eyes.

"Oh! I know you are as true as steel," she said. "If we are meant to meet again, the way will be cleared. Now let us part. Shall I write to you from Paris?"

"Oh, by Jove, yes!—*please*, Flora. Arun House, Park Lane, don't you know? Too big a place, by Jove! for a bachelor. There's Arundel—a dozen times as rich as I —lives in a cosy corner in the Albany—snug as a squirrel in an old rotten tree. Wish he'd change."

Lord Arun and Mrs. Trevor walked to the gates of the pier together, and there parted. Neither was quite satisfied. Flora —but for one imminent, perhaps inevitable, danger—might at once be Lady Arun. She liked both Arun and his title. As to him, he was very decidedly in love, but had not resolve enough to break down all barriers, and force the lady to a confession. He saw in Flora a creature very different from what she really was, and he, of course, believed in the perfect innocence and purity of his own creation.

In the course of the day he sought Lifton, to arrange about the journey to London.

Arundel Lifton was in one of his least amiable moods. He had been watching the flirtation between Lord Arun and Mrs. Trevor, and thought it went on too slowly. There was a point at which he meant to intervene—not precisely like the Queen's Proctor—and that point they seemed to take a long time to reach. He felt himself in the position of a man who waits for the *dénouement* of a comedy which declines to arrive.

"Yes," he said, in reply to Lord Arun's inquiry; "I have ordered horses on. We'll drive four-in-hand all the way. I'm tired of Brighton, Val, but I hate the idea of London. Of course, you'd never tire of Brighton, with that little widow here. Have you made up your mind about her?"

"She's going to Paris," said Lord Arun.

"And a very good place for her," quoth Lifton. "She's quite the Palais Royal style. Do you like her very much, Val?"

"I—'pon honour, you know—never saw anybody I could like half—pooh! a thousandth as much."

"Val," said Lifton, "although you're a peer of the realm, you're a young muff. Be logical. Mrs. Trevor is—heaven knows whom. She confesses herself a widow. She is some years older than you. She wanders from place to place without any definite abode. Why can't you think of Sarum's daughter? She'll be a peeress in her own right, and have all the Sarum estates, and she's very pretty and very clever. I believe she likes you a little. Don't let that flirting little widow entrap you into something foolish."

"She's—by Jove!—the best little woman in the world!" said Arun vehemently.

"All right, my dear boy," said Lifton. "You will know women better when you are a few years older. Whether you will be glad to have obtained that knowledge I cannot say. I have not been much delighted at what I have learnt."

"Oh, that be hanged!" exclaimed Arun. "By Jove, you know, a world without women wouldn't do. It would be like—like a cigar-case without weeds, don't you see? And as to widows—I say, Arundel, couldn't we have an Act to make their first marriage null and void, don't they call it?"

"I should think the death of the husband sufficed for that," said Lifton. "Come, Arun, forget your widow. Let her go to Paris first, and the mischief afterwards. What *can* it matter? There are both widows and maidens ready to snap at your coronet, with its appendages of coin. Forget your Flora."

"Never!" said Arun, "never!"—which is exactly what Arundel Lifton wanted him to say.

CHAPTER XX.

FORNCETT'S DEN.

O that I had the wings of a dove!
DAVID, Rex.

Give me again my hollow tree,
A crust of bread, and liberty!
POPE, Poëta.

MAN has many affinities with the world, which was created to give him enjoyment and suffering, to give him the development designed to result in completion elsewhere. The world is full of life and meaning: not a flower or insect but has its special service to render to the Lord of Earth, the creature made in the Creator's image, the heir of a universe. The infinite possibility of sin, which causes the weak to shudder at the imaginable degradation of the race, is more than balanced by an infinite possibility of virtue. More than balanced, we maintain—since strength is greater than weakness, as God is greater than Satan: and one Carlyle or Ruskin rescues humanity from the shame of having produced a hundred Napoleons or Ortons. One ruddy rose. compensates a thousand weeds: one dog, all friendliness and daring, makes you pardon efts and frogs and slugs for existing. May not the race of man be similarly estimated ?

Most of us have felt the royal poet's desire to take swift wings and fly to some inaccessible solitude, nearer to the Deity—far beyond the reach of the crowd's turmoil. As the carrier pigeons career around the gables of this cottage, as the tumblers rise into ether for the sake of suddenly dropping into the depth, who would not be emulous of them? But the agile and unprisonable spirit of man can climb the silver stair of air to divine heights, where wings could not float. Hence, when the babble of life is most childish, the imagination can seek a quiet home, irradiated by the central light.

Alas! one's imagination is not always in good working order: then a man may be forgiven for desiring tangible wings—wings strong enough to overcome the power of gravitation, and to land one on some pure peak untrodden except by voyaging angels. On the other hand, there is sometimes a just opposite desire—a longing to imitate the squirrel with his store of nuts and acorns in his hollow tree, to hibernate in a library corner with store of books, and pens and ink, and wine—there to "chew the cud of sweet and bitter fancies." A strange delight lurks in such a solitude. The world's vain outcry is unheard. You read no newspapers or maudlin magazines. Ancient poetry and philosophy surround you. If the world is inventing a new religion or making a new war it matters not to you. The hours pass in reverie: essay or poem may perchance grow slowly beneath your pen. In such solitude it is easier than elsewhere to attack some philosophic problem which baffled Pythagoras, or to conjure bright-haired Apollo from his home at Delos, and steal his music for some lovely myth. Goddesses flutter through the student's lonely chamber, and the odour of immortal amaranth floats on the air.

Both these antagonist moods did Frank Forncett love to gratify. He had wandered far and wide; he thought that he should wander no longer. When a wild mood seized him, Ralph saddled Grum, and away he flew for a good gallop. This satisfied him for awhile : now he could retreat to his chimney-corner, read, and write margin-notes in his favourite books—dream the dreams of a man whose youth-vision of life has departed long ago, fading like a rainbow into a watery sky. Frank Forncett, having decided that he had no future, claimed a right to use the present in his own way for his own delight.

Although upon the high road, Forncett's new demesne was snugly fenced. Evergreens grew thickly, screening him when he chose to stroll along a path which ran round his lawn. At the back also he was beyond inquisitive eyesight: the gardens and green-houses had a pleasant privacy, though you could see from them across miles of meadow and wheat-field. It was the very place wherein a country mouse might vegetate.

Now Mr. Temple's place, just opposite,

had been thrown more open to the road than ever before by the destructive Mrs. Selfe, and was noticeable by Forncett as he strolled up and down, well screened by his Portugal laurels. He saw its calm and dignified master ride out in the forenoon, sometimes with his daughter as companion. He watched Kate Temple, a pretty wilful thing, flying about the garden, or riding her pony in the orchard, or tripping across the road to post letters at Miss Tattleton's. Kate Temple was a pleasant study to Forncett. The easy ways of an unconscious girl have a magical charm. This child, with heart untouched, with "life in every limb," with eyes like Sakhrat, that gives the sky its colour (wondrous old myth!) was a delight to look upon. In her, as Wordsworth wrote, Nature had trained a lady of her own. She was in all things simple as a rivulet, natural as a sunbeam. Forncett, who loved all beautiful beings, watched her delightedly, himself unseen.

Of the third occupant of Winterslow his glimpses were rare and remote. The tall dark lady never left the grounds : she passed swiftly from the front garden to the higher grounds above, and was especially fond of a little wood whence she could see for miles across the country. Forncett, who loved the study of mysteries, wondered why she thus secluded herself: and his interest in the question was intensified by the fact that her figure and walk seemed to remind him of some one—well, there is always *some one* to every man.

Frank Forncett was a casuist. He had decided that, as the screen of Portugal laurels had been planted by some former dweller in his house, he had a perfect right to use it for watching the village. So he looked at the passers-by with a clear conscience. None of them interested him enough to make him doubtful of the morality of his position. He liked to see Kate cantering her pony; he liked to see the farmers pass to market; he liked all forms of life on the highway. But, when he looked at the elder lady of Winterslow, shyly crossing the garden to reach the upper solitude she loved, there was something in her walk that seemed familiar to him. A good field-glass lay on his table : in a moment he could tell whether she was, as he fancied strangely, some one whom he knew, or ought to know; but he could not decide in his mind that it was right to use that glass. Had his naked eye told him who the lady was, there would have been no harm; but to level a field glass at her, and bring her simulacrum close to him, when she evidently desired concealment, seemed to him dishonourable. There was the glass on the table;

there, gazing eastward on the reflection of
a superb sunset, stood the lady, at the
entrance to the wood. It was in his power
at once to solve the painful problem, to
ascertain whether she was in any way
known to him. But he decided that he
would not do it.

Men like Frank Forncett, lovers of travel
and of solitude, are always superstitious. All
men of genius are superstitious, in the true
meaning of that much-warped word. Forncett had surely as good a right to a demon
as Socrates himself: and he began to believe that his demon had led him to Copse
Hill with intent to solve the mystery of his
life. That solution seemed to him imminent.
But he would not hurry it, even by lifting a
field-glass to his eye. He would not ask a
question. He would wait. When you
have got a downright perplexity, that has
lasted from youth upward, you are loth to

part with it. Your old enemy, by long acquaintanceship, becomes a friend. A man who has nursed a mystery or an agony for a score of years feels that he would not be the same man without it. The inference is that such matters are best left alone. Take the world easily.

Precisely. Frank Forncett had resolved to take the world easily. Here he was, in his hollow tree, with a fine store of books to read and of wine to drink. What more could he want? Yet his favourite volumes lay untouched, and his dinner was sometimes unenjoyed, because he could not decide that he had a right to point his field glass at a certain lady who wandered in the opposite grounds, and whose movements, as she wandered, brought back to him strange memories of a time of wild delight followed by bitter regret.

CHAPTER XXI.

APRIL FOOLS.

Beauty grows lovelier and youth more flighty
In April, month of flowers and Aphrodite.

JACK SEBRIGHT did not get over his sudden restlessness. He had now a double difficulty in his life. Hitherto his mind had been much perplexed by the problem of his career. *Could* he become a clergyman, uncertain as he felt of his own fitness, unsettled as to his orthodoxy, and perceiving that many great lights of the Church were decidedly dishonest? This question occupied him perpetually: for he had a loving wish to gratify his father, and he sometimes fancied that his scruples must be the result of wrongheadedness or stupidity.

Poor Jack! As if this trouble were not enough for him, he had felt something like a sudden electric shock, which had made the blood tingle in all his arteries—which had made his nerves tremulous as an Æolian harp wind-smitten. He could not understand it. He had known heaps of girls—very charming girls; notably Diana and Claudia. He delighted in their company, but it was not a painful delight, a pleasure touched with ' fear. Now, suddenly and strangely, one glimpse of a girl who was probably much like other girls seemed to have stung him through. What could it mean?

> " Poison they said it was. I too have drunk of it,
>   This is the passionate poison of love,"

says the pale Pachinitzka in one of Lord Lytton's Servian songs. Jack Sebright had no kind adviser to explain this to him.

Those who know best the magical impulse of love will see most clearly how Jack Sebright, a pure and thoughtless young fellow, might be stricken with the malady without knowing quite what it meant. He connected it with Kate Temple, of course; he could not well help that, for the permanent notion in his head was a desire to see her gay young beauty again. Next morning, after breakfast, he wandered away upon the moorland, gay with the yellow furze which always blooms when kissing is in season. He walked a mile or two into the most solitary part; then, at a spot where one silver-rinded birch hung its leafless boughs over a clear spring, he threw his massive young limbs on the grass, and tried hard to think out his position.

Had he been a poet, a philosopher, or a man of the world, it is easy to see how the reverie would have ended : either would have satisfied himself, with the help of a lyric, an apophthegm, or a cigar, that he was worthy to win any lady in the world. Jack, being neither of these, but only a healthy boy, slow of growth, without experience and without conceit, was unable to deal with his difficulty in this prompt pleasant way.   Plays and romances were to him mere rubbish, so that he had not discovered the tremendous force of sexual magnetism. He had not, to use Clough's phrase, "studied the question of sex."   He had regarded girls as sisters and playmates—creatures to be looked on with admiration and treated tenderly.   It was not so very long since he had been skating with Diana and Claudia in mere gaiety of heart; and now just one glimpse of a girl unknown to him had awakened an unconquerable tumult in his soul.

There was music all around to calm his perturbed spirit. A light wind rustled the birch boughs. The slight overflow of the spring tinkled over the stones in its runnel. A lark showered down his sparkling silver melody. A daring bullfinch, perched on the very summit of a tall rose-brier amid the furze, poured out his voluble flutings. These things soothed the young fellow somewhat, and a pleasant vision came to him of Kate Temple, as he had seen her but yesterday, a new Aphrodite, brighter and daintier than the old—being born of the air instead of the sea. His manhood stirred within him; he felt that there was a new glory in life—an aim that made nobler all other aims. He could not have put into any words the thoughts which coursed through him in that hour of solitude; only it seemed that the music of the lark and bullfinch, tree and rivulet, blended into the song of a divine young voice—a voice he had never heard.　Was he right, I wonder? Was Kate Temple singing, light of heart— and had the magic music power to reach his ear?

Any way, Jack Sebright picked himself up like a giant refreshed, and strode away across the heath singing—very much out of tune—some college song about the univer- sity boat-race, quite unsuitable to the fair theme of his thought.　But he felt he must make a noise of some sort, and so he startled the solitude with a pæan of victory sung at " wines " when the Dark Blue had been foremost.

Well, the next day, which chanced to be the first of April, our young friend thought it would be good for his mare and himself that he should have another ride.　I fear he made an April fool of his venerated mother by saying that he had not quite decided which way he should take.

"You should not call to see Mr. Frowde too often," said Mrs. Sebright. "A gentleman so much engaged as he is cannot afford to waste time upon idle visitors. And you really should not miss your lunch so often, my dear boy: you require nutritious and regular food."

"I always can get bread and cheese and ale at a wayside inn," replied Jack.

"But you said the ale about here was so very bad," she remonstrated. "Hadn't you better take some sandwiches and a flask of sherry?"

On this precaution, indeed, Mrs. Sebright insisted—having a deep conviction that Jack was delicate, though he was sound as a roach and hard as nails. After all, even the most Herculean youngster that ever breathed need not be ashamed of the coddling of a too-apprehensive mother. Young fellows who are apt to neglect their mothers should be set to read the immortal apotheosis of motherhood in the Homeric Hymn to Demeter.

So Jack Sebright, armed with sandwich-box and sherry-flask, armed also with the magic power of a new-born love, started forth on Bessie in gayer spirits than those of yesterday. Although he professed uncertainty as to his intentions, either Bessie or he showed great decision of purpose, and Copse Hill was reached by the shortest possible route. He apologized much to Frowde for looking him up again so soon; but the fine weather had tempted him to ride, and he thought the road to Copse Hill the pleasantest in the neighbourhood.

"Always glad to see you," said Frowde. "When I'm busy I shall say so, and you can talk to the missus, if she isn't busy also, or you can take a book, and stroll about the lawn and read. As to what you say about the road, there is this question : how far does your idea of the beauty of a road depend on what you expect at the end of it?"

" I expected some wise talk, and I have got it already," quoth Jack, with unusual readiness.

" Wise talk by itself is like the apples of the Dead Sea," said the other. " And I don't think you particularly want to be talked to just now. You want to think for yourself, slowly. The soul should move like a star, unhasting, unresting. Be in no hurry with the problems of life, Sebright."

Jack hardly knew whether or not his friendly adviser had found out the new problem which perplexed him. There was a tone in Frowde's voice which seemed significant. After all, his friend perhaps was only thinking of Jack's difficulty about his career.

He made no reply.

"Our gay friends Diana and Claudia are coming for a week at Easter," resumed Frowde. "You must ride over and help us to entertain them. You, as a possible parson, doubtless know that Easter will be here in ten or twelve days."

"I shall be delighted to come," said Jack. "The Miss Selfes are most charming young ladies."

Frowde and his friend were at the gate, close to the high road. They looked round at the sound of horses' hoofs. Mr. Temple and his daughter rode by homewards, exchanging bows with Frowde: and Jack Sebright caught one gay bright glance from Kate, which, like a flash of lightning, shot through his eyes to the inner citadel of his soul. Some moments passed before he could hear what Frowde was saying.

"You should have been here yesterday. You missed a chance. I made acquaintance with Mr. and Miss Temple. She is very charming, though you did not seem to think much of her when we saw her the other day."

Jack inwardly execrated.

" She ran all over the lawn here, like the pretty gay child she is, and sang scraps of song as spontaneously as the skylark sings."

Jack thought of the magic music on the moor yesterday, and wondered whether it could have been the remote echo of Kate Temple's voice.

"I must start now," he said abruptly, looking at his watch. " I promised to be home early."

"Remember Easter," said Frowde. " You must not disappoint Diana and Claudia. And I daresay we shall see a good deal of the Temples. But come over here whenever you have time."

Jack rode away, rapidly at first, but

slowly enough when he got into the green soft solitary lanes. The light of Kate Temple's eyes had struck him like a sun-shaft, and he was glad to dream of her alone.

"Lucky for that boy," said Frowde to his wife, as he entered his book-room and sat down in the bay-window to work, "that he has fallen in love. It will simplify his previous difficulties."

"We must give him every chance at Easter," she said. "I like him."

This couple thought so much together that they required few words.

Kate Temple had *seen* Jack Sebright when that glance of hers caught him. Hard-ly had she noted him when riding down Copse Hill two days before. Now she had a picture of him—strong, stalwart, fresh, boyish, eager—the youthful making of a knightly man. Kate had never thought much about men, except her father, whom she idolised; she was too healthy to have a pet parson; she had been too wisely and kindly taught by Mr. Temple to fall into romantic silliness of any sort. When she jumped from her pony at the hall door of Winterslow she said,

"Papa, did you notice that young man with Mr. Frowde at his gate?"

"I just caught sight of him. A fine young fellow, rather."

"I thought he looked so boyish and simple for his age," said Kate; "very much as if he had not made up his mind as to the sort of world he had come into."

Mr. Temple laughed, as he often had to laugh at Kate's off-hand judgment of people. She was commonly right. That bright eye of hers did her good service.

"We will talk him over by-and-by," he said. "Find mamma. I want her to see the new fountain play, that we may decide about its height."

The beautiful dark-haired lover of silence and solitude was dreaming over one of Shakespeare's saddest plays when Kate summoned her with a loving kiss, lovingly returned.   She came out reluctantly.

"Leonora," said Mr. Temple, "come down—the grass is not damp—and see the fountain play.   I want your idea as to the height the water should go to look well from the house, without injuring the lilies or disturbing the gold-fish.   You are so good a judge of those things."

She came reluctantly, for she hated being near the high-road, shrinking from the gaze of strangers. She gave her advice, and it was taken.   Then, as soon as possible, she walked away across the lawn, taking Kate's hand in hers, and swinging it to and fro.

"Mamma, you are better to-day," said Kate.

"I am quietly happy, my child," she replied, and kissed her.

Frank Forncett, down behind that screen of Portugal laurels, had been looking on all this time. He had not previously been so close to the lady who troubled him with the ghost of a mysterious memory. Now an idea occurred to him which seemed impossible. As she stood by the margin of that pond, watching the fountain experiment with half concealed indifference—as she took Kate's hand in hers, swinging it gaily as they went briskly up the slope—as she stooped to kiss her, like a goddess in the movement—Forncett was more and more convinced, more and more puzzled.

He walked out into the road. She had gone. He strolled downward, and met Frowde, with a huge bundle of letters, going to the post. They exchanged a few words, about nothing in particular. Then Forncett said,

"Our neighbours at that bay-windowed house—do you know their names?"

"Temple," said Frowde.

"*Temple!* Do you know what the family is?"

"Mr., Mrs., and Miss Temple," said Frowde, "and very nice people they seem to be."

"And you are sure one of the ladies is Mrs. Temple?"

"I see no reason to doubt it," said Frowde. "Her daughter is a charmingly fresh little girl. Forgive me—here is the postman : and I have a lot of foreign stamps to get."

Frank Forncett walked back to his own house, and Ralph opened the door to him, seeing him from that sanctum which commanded a view of the front gate.

"Ralph," he said, "do you know anything about those people at Winterslow?"

"Name's Temple, your honour."

"Yes, so I hear. What's their relation? Husband and wife, brother and sister, or what? Find that out for me, if you can."

"If I can!" quoth Ralph, disdainfully. "I'll find out anything your honour wants, if I've to climb Mont Blanc or go down Vesuvius. I'll inquire at once."

And away went Ralph, whispering thus to himself:

"Now what's the matter with the master? He never cared to know who's who before. Please God he isn't in love with either of them. I don't want a woman to manage. He's trouble enough."

And Frank Forncett was saying to himself: "It must be she. No other woman ever had that walk of dignity and grace. How is she here? What means the adoption of the name of Temple? Who is the man? And is the girl her daughter? I must know, for I'll swear she is Leonora."

CHAPTER XXII.

SHOOLING.

Qui dies mensem Veneris marinæ
Findit Aprilem.

EASTER fell about the Ides of April. Diana and Claudia were to spend it at Copse Hill, taking a pleasant round from place to place, as they travelled. This custom is known as "shooling" in the North Country. The phrase is used by sailors for getting into shallow water when the shore slopes safely and by degrees. The sisters did their shooling in a wise and enjoyable way: their pony Rough took them very comfortably from place to place in a vehicle which may perhaps be described as a lady's dog-cart. They were as independent in their movements as Arundel Lifton in his four-in-hand—possibly safer, though there is a rumour that Claudia once let Rough down when reading a letter of extreme interest. From whom? I wonder.

What a delicious April morning it was! Only a few white feathery clouds floated above the round tower of Avonside Castle, which rises in historic grandeur opposite the quaint farm-cottage that has been nick-named the Doll's House. All the rest of the sky is blue, and a myriad martlets, "oiseaux de retour," are eddying high in air. Diana and Claudia, agile and succinct, with their pretty heads full of adventure impossible, bade farewell to servitor and servitress, and to Rory, the cleverest and most amiable of collies, and gave Rough his head. That sagacious pony, who had heard the gay chatter and rippling laughter of his young mistresses, knew well that there was something up. He was not going to the railway-station this time, he knew. He shook his head wisely and trotted merrily, and made light of the roads, which were clogged with clay that a tropical sun could scarcely dry.

As we watch these daring damsels starting to "shool," we cannot help wishing them some lively adventures. Highwaymen are extinct—so are knights errant; so are troubadours. Diana and Claudia both had courage enough to dance a minuet with Claud du Val. That most chivalrous of thieves has been hanged long ago; and, although the Premier maintains that "adventures are to the adventurous," we doubt whether Don Quixote himself could find much adventure on our well-policed English roads. When it does come, it is of too vulgar a sort to be pleasant.

To walk through England is delightful: the man who can take a month to do his devious twenty miles a-day will get more enjoyment than the traveller who rushes to look for Prester John and the Troglodytes during his brief holiday. Eagerness to traverse great distances and see strange places is a symptom of that anxiety to escape from oneself—the inseparable companion one most hates—which Lucretius describes. The pessimist must, logically, hate himself, and wish himself at—say Jericho: but no, Jericho is the City of Flowers, and your pessimist is a weed—mind and matter out of their place. We, being optimist, believe in ourself, and believe that there is no place like England for travel.

From Doll's House to Copse Hill is seventy miles, and Rough promised to do it in three days. The first day was uneventful. The weather was charming: they found a tolerable village inn at night, with the customary refreshment of eggs and bacon; and there were some ancient volumes of novels in the rather stuffy parlour, with which they read themselves into a somnolent state. Now and then they burst into laughter as some scene more tenderly or terrifically ridiculous than usual turned up: and then they commonly exchanged volumes, and mixed their tales; so that, as Claudia remarked, it was sometimes impossible to know what finally happened. Diana, who has a knack at epigram, pencilled on a flyleaf—

" Thanks, volumes dear to servant girls,
  To ease their brains and twist their curls,
  You've given us an hour of laughter—
  I hope no hideous dreams hereafter.
  Of you we don't at all complain :
  You sell small beer, and not champagne.
  When Ouida, wonder of her sex,
  Declares her tap is Treble X—
  When flighty Broughton, flavorous Braddon . . ."

At this moment, while Diana was deciding whether *gladden, sadden,* or *madden,* was the proper rhyme, in came the servant with bed-room candles. Diana shut the book suddenly, and made an awful smudge. But her inestimable autograph poem, though blurred and unfinished, remains; and many a wayfarer, solacing himself with bread and cheese and beer and books at the sign of the Hog and Nutcrackers, will wish that he could see more of the works of so charming a poetess.

To-morrow morning. Eggs and bacon again. Such food becomes monotonous. On, therefore—with certainty that, if it be eggs and bacon all this day also, the next will bring Copse Hill and rumpsteak,—possibly oysters. The sisters pass through the loveliest city in the world : even Rough feels poetical as he sees the wondrous towers and spires unparagoned, and climbs

"The streamlike windings of the glorious street."

But here they stay not. They have heard of a fascinating wayside inn, four or five miles on, which has a quaint, courteous landlord, a comely and homely landlady, and something to eat beyond the product of the pullet and the pig. Onward they fare, joyously and hungrily (let us not say thirstily, lest we libel ladies), and are thinking how jolly it will be, when all at once capricious April comes down with a sudden windy deluge of rain that so astonishes Rough as to make him pull up short.

"This is a judgment on you, Di," said Claudia, "for writing rubbish in that poor man's book. We can't stop there again."

"We won't stop here, at any rate," said Diana, flagellating Rough, who had made up his mind that the flood had come a second time, and that the best thing was to stand still and bear it.

The drenched damsels reached the Courtenay Arms at last;—such a poetic hostelry; an active ostler of evident Irish descent, who understood Rough's idiosyncrasy at a glance; a ruddy landlord, who took a fatherly interest in the young ladies, and brought them at once into a room where a grand fire was burning, as if expectant of two girls who wanted to be dried; best of all, the kindliest and most humorous of landladies, a little woman in old-fashioned costume, who made them change their clothes with a pleasant despotism, and asked them what they would like for dinner.

"Anything but eggs and bacon," said Claudia promptly.

"Eggs and bacon are very nice," said the little old landlady, "supposing the eggs to be well-fed and fresh, and the bacon also well-fed and toasted to a turn. But we can give you something nicer than that. My master was thinking that a trout and a veal cutlet or so and a couple of roast pigeons might suit two young ladies on their travels; and I've got store of jelly and marmalade and other nice things—my own making, every one of them—that you'll like for dessert."

" We're in clover," said Diana, when the landlady had left. " We shall have to stop here again. I only hope they won't charge us immense prices for this fairy-like dinner. Only fancy, Claudia—trout! after that ever-lasting bacon and eggs."

" Yes; and marmalade! I do hope its quince marmalade, made from their own trees. It must be, for the old lady has quite a fruity look about her. I declare I'm very hungry."

The dinner did not disappoint them. The trout was delicious; the pigeons were perfect; the marmalade was quince of Oxfordshire, not orange of Seville. They had as handmaid a bright-eyed neat-handed Phillis, who stared much at them when she got an opportunity, without, as she imagined, being found out. But there were a couple of old mirrors in the room, and, as she knew nothing about angles of incidence and reflection, they caught sight of her wide mouth and perplexed eyes at intervals, and laughed quietly. And when dessert was on the table—delectable home-made cakes and delicacies—the landlord appeared, and hoped they had dined well, and asked if they would like a glass of perry, made by a brother of his in Herefordshire.

"It isn't champagne, ladies, you know—but I like it better; and the young sparks from college, they like it better; and I don't see why a good English pear shouldn't give as fine a drink as a foreigneering grape."

With which prologue he opened the sparkling fluid ; and Diana and Claudia enjoyed the same beverage which delighted Coningsby and Sidonia in merry Sherwood. Certes, perry is a glorious drink, and I am surprised that Englishmen, who will swallow hideous nastiness because it is labelled champagne, will not touch the wines made from native fruits. Happy is that man who can enjoy good cider.

The Courtenay Arms gave our shoolers a cup of tea. Then, as they sat by the welcome fire, wondering what weather it would be to-morrow, Claudia said,

"I am willing to bet there is not a novel in this hostelry."

"I should think not," replied Diana. "I wonder what there is. Heighho! I am too lazy to look."

She leant back in her chair, her bright hair rippling over fair shoulders, and looked a picture of laziness. Dark-haired Claudia was quite as bad. They did not hunt for books that night.

The fire burned warm and red, enjoyable in a damp midnight of April. Diana and Claudia were in happy reverie, now and then broken by a word or two of chat. At length one said,

" Let's go to bed."

And the other replied,

" Let's——"

At that very moment they heard six shots fired with the utmost rapidity. They started up from their chairs. All the horrors they had ever read in their youth of dreadful murders in mysterious inns curdled their young blood. They had not energy enough to rush into each other's arms for mutual protection. While undecided whether to faint or ring the bell, the door opened, and there entered a light young man in a light overcoat, with a light and airy way about him, the landlord following.

"I have only just heard," the light young man said, "that I may have alarmed you, ladies. I was surrounded by a gang of tramps, who tried to rob me. I always carry weapons, so I fired a revolver in the air, and off they ran. I trust you were not much startled."

"We were in search of adventures," said Claudia.

"And I was in search of Balliol College, where I am offered a philosophical bed," he rejoined. "But this is too comfortable a corner to quit—the translator of Plato shall wait for me, and I'll sleep in mine host's hay-loft if beds are scarce."

The girls were very happy to have so jolly a comrade unexpectedly. The landlord found him a succulent supper, and he drank the perry most joyously.

"I am an unfortunate man," he said, eating his impromptu supper as if he were not at all unfortunate; "I can't go anywhere without an adventure. From the very first day of my existence, when my infant scream caused the apprehension of a burglar, I have had no day without an extraordinary incident of some sort. Nobody but I, walking to Oxford to listen to metaphysics, would have been driven by a gang of tramps into happy converse with two charming ladies. This is a day to be marked with white chalk."

"You always have adventures?" said Diana.

"Always. Generally, good comes of them. I have detected several scoundrels, and made two or three people happy. I fancy there is some electricity in me which bring events to a point—crystallizes them, one may say. But how confoundedly I talk about myself! Do you ladies meet with no adventures?"

"Nothing worse than rain," said Diana. "We are shooling: do you know what that means?"

"Of course I do; looking in upon your friends as you zigzag through the world. Awful fun. So you are doing it now? Where next, if it is not wicked to ask?"

"Copse Hill—Mr. Frowde's," said Claudia.

"Frowde! By Jove, is his place so near? I want to see him about a literary matter. Are you going to spend Easter there? Tell him I'll come in a day or two."

"Who shall we tell him will come," said Diana.

"Oh! I'm nobody. Tell him Tix will come. You pass through Bix on your way. "Don't confuse them. You'll not mind carrying a Bohemian message to the ex-King of Bohemia?"

"I shall remember," said Claudia; "Tix will come. If Tix breaks his promise he will forfeit all pretension to chivalry."

The light young patrician rose, and wished them good night, saying to Claudia with a smile:

"You can read character."

Next day was radiant. They saw nothing of their overnight acquaintance. The landlord and lady of the Courtenay Arms started them with great glee: all the idlers of the village came to see them mount their dog-cart. A pleasant road, and, to the delight of Rough, chiefly down hill. They passed through a village with a famous church, which was a city and the centre of a great bishopric a thousand years ago; they ate mutton chops at an inn eight hundred feet above the sea level, which is something to boast of when you are not near the Alps; they went down hill, through avenues of fir, till they reached the most ancient town in the county, situated on a delightful reach of the Thames, and then it was but six miles to Copse Hill. There they arrived, without accident or adventure or shower, just long enough before dinner to put themselves in perfect order.

"There is no particular news," said Manly Frowde, when they sat down to dinner. "Your mamma has gone; the new vicar has arrived, and seems a very good fellow; Jack Sebright has not yet made up his mind about anything; the new people at your old place are pleasantly mysterious."

"And everybody still gossips," said Mrs. Frowde.

END OF THE FIRST VOLUME.

LONDON : PRINTED BY DUNCAN MACDONALD, BLENHEIM HOUSE.

www.ingramcontent.com/pod-product-compliance
Lightning Source LLC
Chambersburg PA
CBHW031029120726
47905CB00007B/2102